IN HOT WATERS

Flavien Desoblin

IN HOT WATERS. Copyright © 2014 by Flavien Desoblin, with C. Chamberlain & Bridger Redmond. Edited by Catherine Foulkrod.

ISBN: 0991464702
ISBN 13: 9780991464708
Library of Congress Control Number: 2014933173
Congeners Press, New York, NY

To my inspiring uncles
Serge and Gaël

Prologue

The New York Times
July 15, 2010
Speculation, and Clues, about Unearthed Ship

*T*wo *days after construction workers discovered the keel of a centuries-old wooden ship at the site of the new World Trade Center, New Yorkers continued to speculate...*

Hundreds of readers weighed in about the ship on the City Room blog. Some fretted that it might have ferried human cargo. Others were convinced that it was a whaling ship. The whaling enthusiasts were confident, asserting that a metal arc found on the keel, not far from some loose bricks, might have once belonged to an [explosive] fixture that helped sailors process blubber.

Meanwhile, city officials said Thursday that additional clues had surfaced since the keel was found Tuesday at a site bounded by Liberty Street to the north and Cedar Street to the south.

Among the new finds: an anchor located near the ship, and some spikes that might help pinpoint the age of the vessel.

Archaeologists who examined the ship were confident that it was deliberately placed in the ground as landfill back when Lower Manhattan was expanding in several directions. They say New Yorkers threw anything they no longer needed into these cavernous projects, from discarded cherry pits to old shoes and animal horns.

Amanda Sutphin, the director of archaeology for the city's Landmarks Preservation Commission, said she believed that the vessel had been retired in the late 18th century. Maps as far back as 1797 show a newly-created Washington

Street weaving its way over the site where the ship was unearthed. "By 1800, there was a street on top of where it was found," Ms. Sutphin said.

—Alison Leigh Cowan

Not reported: A liquor bottle with its original contents was discovered near the hull.

The morning Earl Barclay found the bottle, it was raining. He arrived on the construction site, his usual egg and cheese on a roll from the corner bodega in tow, a cup of coffee in hand. Never an umbrella man, Barclay wore a thick black raincoat, hood up. He walked fast, efficiently unlocking the construction trailer's door, and stepping into the dry, quiet space. He had arrived early that day, hoping to sift through the paperwork that had amassed on his desk since the ship had been found, and it would be at least an hour before his excavation crew or the archaeologists arrived. Barclay was not a paper pusher. He moved earth. But for the past several days, his backhoes had been at a standstill, their mechanical shovels replaced by a team of archaeologists from the Landmarks Preservation Commission who moved dirt in miniature with brushes and trowels, buckets and brooms, cordoning artifacts with grids of nylon cord.

Barclay looked out the half-fogged window of the trailer that morning and felt thankful for the rain. The earth was a deep, rutted gray, stoic and heavy looking, and the moisture dampened the retch of sulfur and sea brine that rose from the sludge. Barclay took a sip of coffee and shifted his gaze toward the white tarps the archaeologists had set up to protect the ribcage of the centuries-old hull. The wind had dislodged one at the corner, and a stream of water ran underneath.

Barclay had not considered himself a man to tamper with history, or one to disrupt the integrity of an archaeological dig. He had no intention of touching, let alone taking, anything he saw underneath that loose flap. He only meant to take a quick glance before he refastened the tarp. Careful to crouch outside of the grid, Barclay took a visual survey of the rotting wood, tiny flags diligently numbering each plot. But when he looked at the ground to find the stake that had come loose, in a small moat of rain just outside the dig's boundary, he noticed a glint of glass the rain had washed clean.

Barclay's phone buzzed, startling him. He froze, then remembered himself and pulled out the cell. "Might as well shoot the whole day in the ass," his foreman blurted without a hello.

"I'll call you back in ten," Barclay replied, and shoving the phone back into his coat, he lowered to one knee and put a hand into the earth.

CHAPTER ONE

One week later, miles uptown, a phone was ringing. Samuel Dugranval ignored it and turned the knife over in his palm. Only one man alive knew how to open this switchblade, and it was not him. He studied the weapon, inspecting its thuya burl handle for an irregularity, for anything that might reveal its trick. Like his wife, only a certain combination of fiddling could make her release, and, *God, it's beautiful.*

A gift from a fellow inquisitor of nature's materials (water, stone, wood, *especially wood*), this knife had been handcrafted exclusively to fit his palm and came equipped with a locking device that could not be sprung open without directions from the maker himself. But that maker was thousands of miles away in the Cognac region of France, letting Samuel sweat it out across the pond in New York City. It would be days, if not weeks, before instructions arrived.

The phone let out a final protest, then went mum.

"Come on beauty, loosen up," Samuel whispered to the knife. "Show me your secrets…"

A woman cleared her throat. "Talking to yourself again, I see."

He had not heard her come in, and a faint red bloomed up Dugranval's neck. Her voice was saccharine and matronly, and the body standing in the doorway of his cellar-like office matched. Olivia Bordes, known around the lab as Mrs. B., tapped a white envelope against her long, sturdy hip. Her graying hair was fastened in a low ponytail, and a man's button-up shirt worn under an open white lab coat leant her an air of formality that was in contrast to her kind face; a face that was giving Sam an urgent, blue-eyed stare.

1

"No return address," she said, lifting reading glasses to her nose and walking over to Dugranval's desk.

The phone lit up again, rattling for attention.

Sam threw up a hand, gesturing to leave the phone be, and took the envelope from his administrator. "No postage either," he said, and looked over the neatly scripted name on the front of the envelope—his own, followed by the acronym IFDM. The Institute of Fermentation, Distillation, and Maturation. He flipped the envelope over. At first glance, it appeared blank, but when he tilted it in the light, a distinct watermark could be seen. Mrs. B. leaned over his shoulder, nosing in.

"Kanji," he said.

The woman's eyes widened. "Do you think?"

"Not this quickly. The case was only filed yesterday. There's no way those Japanese crooks could know." And yet Samuel's body stiffened when he thought of the black-market importers with their high-stake threats and short designer suits, whose inevitable coercion he'd surely have to endure once they'd been informed he was the expert witness slated to prove the "premium whiskey" they trafficked was, in fact, synthetic hooch. "The Bureau of Alcohol, Tobacco, and Firearms assured me they'd keep my identity private until the trial," he said, as if to convince himself all was under control.

Something exploded outside the room.

Mrs. B. involuntarily jumped, then rushed out, the bottles shelved by the door rattling in her wake. Moments later, a young man with blond hair—a patch of it singed—came running in. "Too much cock in the fight on that batch," sputtered David Dubehash, Sam's wide-eyed and gangly teaching assistant. The door slammed behind him, and Dugranval's framed master's degree in the business of wine and spirits from the Business School of Dijon, France, fell to the floor. David hurriedly picked it up and rehung it next to a diploma in distilling from the Institute of Brewing and Distilling in the UK.

"It's going to take you a week to get that smell out of your hair, David," Sam said scarcely glancing up, his gaze fixed on the letter. There was another thing: the Japanese owned him. IFDM was heavily funded by several major Japanese distilleries, one of which happened to be

2

the prosecution in an impending whiskey-swapping case. The school had been conceived five years earlier in Japan by way of drunken serendipity involving the Master Distiller of Yamazaki, a recently acquired American distillery's failed run, and some loosening up of all parties in a Geisha house. Rumor had it, upon tasting the botched bourbon, the Master Distiller of Yamazaki had given an impromptu drunken speech in which he called all Americans donkeys and resolved to teach the world how distilling should be done. He'd waxed on about how bourbon was the true American spirit, the wild bravery behind the American West, how it was the wit (and tit) of the South. What had once been a family pride—so much so that bourbons were known only by family name (none named Yamazaki)—had gone the crude way of American mass production. And though Dugranval was employed to pick up the American slack, it went without saying that he'd best bust his ass to protect the Japanese craft as well.

God, David's hair stinks. "David, do you read Japanese?"

"No."

"Didn't think so. Get out of here and help Mrs. B. clean up. You smell like a Shriners hospital."

David made a motion for the door, but lingered, eyeing first the letter, then the knife clenched in Dugranval's fist. "One of Renoux's?" he asked.

Sam nodded and tucked the knife into his blazer. He pushed aside a stack of papers and books—the latest study on the translactones in the Japanese oak Quercus Mongolica, Broom's latest work titled *World Atlas of Whisky*, a rejuvenated *Manuel du Distillateur* 1st edition of 1850 by Delannoy—and put the envelope down. David left.

As if sensing a moment of quiet, the phone rang again. Exasperated, Sam gave in. "Oui?"

"Chicken or fish?" cooed the voice on the line.

"Ah, mon petit lapin." Sam's shoulders relaxed, and his voice softened. "Let's have chicken, dear, we've been cooking so much fish my clothes are beginning to stink."

"Bon, I'll prepare coq au vin," Lydia Dugranval replied. "And..." She paused. "We need to talk tonight. I don't want to bother you now, but Leo's tuition is due, and the donation check for the summer camp bounced."

"Yes." Sam slumped in his seat. "I was expecting that. Listen, dear, we'll figure something out." He sucked in a breath. "Don't worry. David's made a mess over here. I've got to go, but we'll talk later." He cradled the phone and let the breath out, silently cursing the summer camp. *That pool of overbearing mothers and their overprivileged offspring with underdeveloped imaginations and artificial relationships with nature.* "Boh!" He pushed the intercom button, "Mrs. B., please, no more calls today. Forward anything urgent to David."

Samuel looked again at the letter, but he did not touch it. He patted the knife in his pocket but did not pull it out. He scanned the shelves that floor-to-ceiling ensconced him in his office—books and bottles, words and booze—and tried to catch a tenuous thought. A memory Renoux's knife had triggered—the chestnut tree of his Burgundy youth where he and Renoux had spent a summer smashing fingers and blistering hands in pursuit of a tree house. *Yes, the smell of that sturdy wood…*

David whistled outside the office, derailing Sam's train of thought. He was talking vigorously to someone on the phone, and Sam heard a second smaller whistle, then the silence of David listening. Sam stood and headed toward one of the sliding ladders affixed to a brass rail that ran the length of his shelves. *Now where's that little volume on…*

The office door swung open, and David poked his head in. "Hey, Sammy boy, I've got something to cheer you up! A guy named Barclay says he's found whiskey gold. Sounds legit. We're going upstate. Poughkeepsie. I'll fill you in on the way."

CHAPTER TWO

They took the MG Roadster. It was green and fast, with custom wooden floorboards. The upstate woods sped along the roadside, alight with autumn and the brisk, medicinal smell of birch.

David had his legs all over the place.

"David, get your filthy sneakers off my car or I'll give you a taste of my spinning back fist."

David scowled, settling his feet into the foot well. He reached his long arm out and inched the volume down on the car's Bose system, as if by lowering the music he could eke out a few more inches of space.

Sam's mind spun with possibility. "Tell me again what Barclay said. Barclay. That's a Scottish name. I wonder if he's distilling anything in Poughkeepsie."

"He's an excavator," David said. "Said he found the bottle in a ship his crew pulled out from under Ground Zero. He was pretty worked up. It's the deepest they've ever dug there, and the ship's supposedly from the eighteenth century."

"And of course you asked which part of the eighteenth century? Is it a hand-blown sealed bottle, David? I doubt there'd be rum in a bottle on a ship. They'd be drinking that out of casks, so I'm guessing it's Scotch or American rye. But if it was late enough in the century, it could be an early form of bourbon."

"Assuming this bottle came from the United States," David replied.

"Of course," Sam said.

Samuel turned off the Charlie Parker (much to David's delight), adjusted his scarf, and stared at the road. They were on a timeless stretch of highway, no houses visible, and his mind easily drifted back to 1794...

Sam coasted west and past, into the rolling hills of western Pennsylvania where wood smoke rose from thousands of log stillhouses, and Scottish-Irish farmers—the decedents of old-world distillers—cooked up the best rye whiskey in the new world. Crop yields were high, but transportation was slow, and liquor was best way to ship the surplus of grain. These farmer-distillers prospered, but the country was war-broke, in debt, and a new excise tax on booze bore down on all they had. Theirs was a living made by barter, and it was impossible for them to pay the government in cash.

Blame Hamilton. Blame Washington. Tempers soared. Redheaded messengers rode from town to town, rallying against the tax. Rebellion ensued. Sam imagined men dressed up in women's clothing barreling on horses over hills to tar and feather a tax collector; he heard the shouts of a mob threatening to burn Pittsburgh to the ground. Sam thought about Neville, the tax collector whose homestead was torched, his real estate and livestock besieged—and he thought about Washington, how the great general stepped in.

No teetotaler, in fact a distiller himself and a proponent of keeping troops in daily drink, Washington, above all, was a man dedicated to the solidarity of the early United States. The Whiskey Rebellion was a test on the fortitude of the federal government, and Washington seized the opportunity to set a precedent impossible to refute. Atop his steed and dressed in full Revolutionary regalia, Washington mobilized twelve thousand soldiers, and headed personally to confront the rebels.

"God, I love Washington," said Sam.

David laughed. "Man, city, or state?"

"And I love him, not just because of his ties with Lafayette. David, suppose this bottle is the real thing. I think it might have been a personal gift to a rum runner who kept the bottle in the hot waters room in the hull of the ship."

"The captain's personal stash? What makes you think that?"

"This must be it," Sam said, ignoring the question and pointing to a dirt driveway that led to a stone front barn. The front wall of the barn was gray limestone, built from the reclaimed masonry of centuries-old property lines. Samuel could smell the rich soil, alfalfa, the drying of leaves, a landscape preparing for the cold. He rolled down his window to take it all in. *This is some excavator,* he thought. *Someone who obviously has an eye for natural materials.*

A thick-limbed man wearing Carharts and a Shetland wool sweater walked out of the barn. He gestured for Dugranval to park behind a Lincoln Navigator.

"You're lucky it's not raining today," Earl Barclay called out. "Your little MG would get stuck up here." He laughed at his own remark, fierce gray eyes under wild black eyebrows, sparkling with flecks of green. "Just wait until you see what I've got." He thrust his hand at Dugranval as he got out of the car. "The name's Earl."

Samuel and David followed Earl's lead into the post and beam barn. Above them loomed king trusses constructed of hand-hewn white pine. Below them spread a resurfaced concrete floor. The auger of a pellet stove cranked as they entered, feeding more pellets into a fire, illuminating four man-sized Patriot gun safes along the nearest wall. Beyond the safes, a pile of copper—a dismantled moonshiner's still—sat greased with dust.

Barclay followed Dugranval's gaze to the still. "Bought that at a flea ring in Pennsylvania last year," he said. "Haven't had time to set her up."

Dugranval gave an appreciative smile and scraped some dirt off his calfskin shoes. "Where are you keeping the bottle?" he asked.

David readjusted a metal briefcase on his bony hip.

"In my office. This way," said Earl, leading them deeper into the barn. "What's in the case, young man? And what happened to your hair?"

The device in the briefcase was deceptively simple: a long-nosed syringe and three empty-looking vials packed in foam. Dugranval, in collaboration with David at IFDM, had invented the tool as a way of extracting spirits from an unopened bottle without comprising its seal or contents; he would draw out the alcohol with the syringe and replace it with neutral gas using a patented triple-vial, pressure-triggered design.

This little-known technique was born out of Dugranval's frustration with the sensually chaste evaluation methods used across the industry. Several years earlier, when Dugranval was assessing the worth of rare whiskies for Bonham Auction House's annual sale in Hong Kong, he had rebelled. From a chemist's perspective, he appreciated the spectrometric approach that used infrared beams to measure the chemical composition of liquid entombed in glass. But in his gut, Dugranval knew the only true way to put value on a fine spirit was to use his nose and mouth.

"You want to taste it?" asked Barclay, aghast. "Don't you want to run some sort of analysis first?"

Barclay was holding the bottle he had removed from a small safe under his office desk. A free-blown New England chestnut flask, it was a squatty tear drop shape, crudely lipped, and of a thick and bubbled olive-amber glass. No emblem or blot-seal marked its manufacturer or fate; there was only the blowpipe pontil scar at its base.

Authentic, Sam thought.

Barclay grudgingly handed over the bottle.

"It's American made," Sam said and then he pressed the syringe into the cork, delicately, with great precision, hoping he would not damage the theoretically 225-year-old seal. Deep amber-red liquid pooled into the syringe. "This isn't American whiskey," exclaimed Dugranval. "It looks like it came from a Sherry cask. Or, if this is bourbon or rye that was aged in oak, it was most likely aged by accident. No one was aging whiskey in the eighteenth century unless natural maturation was taking place during flatboat transportation. David, look at this coloration!"

Samuel went on for Earl's sake. "See, whiskey distillate is clear when it comes out of the still. At that stage, it's called the 'white dog.' The first thing we teach students about at my institute is oak, the key ingredient that transforms moonshine into whiskey. Well, oak and time. We teach our students everything from cooperage—that's the making of the barrels—to storage—how to best char and store the casks, which species of oak provide the most organoleptically desirable influences. Earl, that just means relating to the senses, but the point is, *oak*. And whatever you have here, it spent years inside a barrel. Are you ready, Mr. Barclay?"

Samuel gave David a nod, and David produced two tulip-shaped glasses that had been packed in foam with the syringe. "Let's see what she's about," Sam said, taking a glass and transferring the liquid from the syringe.

Dugranval closed his eyes. For several minutes, he held completely still, his face hovering over the glass, his hands warming the liquid, mouth slightly open, nostrils flared. His brow furrowed, relaxed, and then he finally began to swirl the contents, lowering his nose into the glass, mouth opening wider and taking in air, his entire countenance settling into a deep repose.

Samuel was a newlywed again, standing in his father-in-law's pâtisserie, his heart in flight. Candied oranges cooled on a tray while sugar and almond extract for marzipan thickened on a stove over low heat. Morning light came through the slightly fogged windows, illuminating wall-sized ovens with convection fans blowing the scents of baking pistachio macarons and pithiviers gateau—flaky pastries filled with almond cream—browning to gold. The aromas were persistent, expanding, hinting of a future intensity, a full-potentialed life.. Somewhere in the back of the shop, crème brûlée was set ablaze, the sweet, burnt scent of sugar caramelizing, and beneath, he caught wafts of butterscotch and baked banana in the air. His wife's leather glove touched his face, and he took in the particular vanilla-like musk of her skin.

Intoxication.

Samuel took his first sip.

Like Jesus in a velvet coat! Samuel's entire palate was draped in a thick and boundless warmth, a liquid thick enough to walk on. And yet the flavors were buoyant and gentle, a carousel of fruit on the tongue: dried apricots and orange marmalade, subtle yet bright, fresh yet never dissipating. Samuel then felt as if he were at his mother's Christmas feast—contentment, wholeness—the apex and culmination of the evening, a table of desserts, a surprising marriage of mint and peach, meringue and marzipan, of laughing faces, and familiar eyes. Citrus candies on waves of oak-tinged caramel, and storied laughs near the fire.

Samuel swallowed.

A fresh spiciness sprung up as the liquid went down. And yet, and yet... it was as if he had never swallowed at all. The fruity aromas grew and intensified retro-nasally as Samuel breathed, lips shut. The finish was locked on his tongue, flavors spreading still, new aromas revealing themselves, something indecipherable, ancient and endless, lingering in the back of his throat.

Minutes passed.

Samuel felt as if he were at mass, awash in the preacher's words, listening, letting them penetrate and inspire from within.

Minutes passed.

Time.

Slowly, imperceptibly, the spirit lifted. Samuel could distinguish its raw materials: corn, oak, and time—the latter two revealing the immenseness of the grain.

David and Earl were staring.

CHAPTER THREE

"**D**id you see me nearly orgasm back there?" Sam said to David in the car, his face in full afterglow. "I would've let you have a taste, but the bottle wasn't mine to share. Plus, there's a little left in the syringe for you, but let's wait until we get back to IFDM."

David was driving the MG. Sam was dialing on his phone. David was gunning it, and there were no cars in sight.

"David, stay in your lane."

"But there are no other cars!"

"Shh. Parker! Hey, old man, if there's anyone who can help me, it's you," Sam nearly shouted into his cell. "I've just tasted something I didn't think could exist. But it does, and I have no idea what *it* is. It's *Usquebaugh*, American style! True water of life, Parker! Only it's blooded. Blood of life."

There was a long pause, and then a back-jawed Kentucky thrush came through the line.

"Slow down, Sam-yull. I have no idea what you are speakin' about. Did you say blooded?"

Parker Beam was the great grandnephew of Colonel James Beauregard Beam, aka Jim Beam, and distilling was in his Kentucky-Scottish blood. He was the Master Distiller at Heaven Hill Distillery, holder of the family recipe, and in Samuel's opinion, the world authority on bourbon.

"Yes, blood. Red-blooded. But it wasn't just the color, Parker, it was the way it lingered on the tongue."

"Son, you are gonna to have to start speakin' straight if you want me to listen. I have a cigar in my hand that hasn't even been lit because of your goings on."

David hit the rumble strip that sent a zooming flutter through the MG.

"David, *steer*! Excuse me, Parker, I'm sorry. I started all wrong. I tasted a whiskey today that was, well, it's beyond words. This stuff is old, as old as the United States. It was corn whiskey, Parker, but it was aged. I'd say ten years at least."

Parker laughed, bit down, and spit. The flint of a lighter was heard. "Sam-yull, you and your glamorous New York City life. Where did you find the stuff?"

"Manhattan. It was dug up in an old boat. I'll tell you the whole story later, but listen, do you still have that research on eighteenth century flatbed transportation? Maybe a barrel got lost some place and sat in a warehouse for too long. I don't know. I can't sit still over here, and I've got to start somewhere. Parker, it's, it's...I've got goose bumps."

"Well, hold-tight there, kiddo. Sure, I still have a file cabinet full of inventory logs." Parker hesitated. "But I never sorted through them, and, well, I must say they are a mess. It will be a mighty laborious task for you to make heads or tails of it all, but my door is always open to you, Sam-yull. You are welcome to come on down here and look through whatever you like."

"Tell Linda to put one of her bourbon pecan pies in the oven. I'm on my way."

CHAPTER FOUR

The first leg of the trip was in first class, and Samuel declined any drink. He didn't want to put anything between him and the memory of what he had just tasted in Poughkeepsie. Among all the precise flavors he recalled, it was the taste of his wife—more accurately, the contented feeling of being with her in the pâtisserie —that came back to him while seated in the faux-leather sterility of the airplane seat. He must have looked slightly strange, sitting with his hand cupped over his mouth and phone, the sack dinner Lydia had dropped off with his suitcase at IFDM resting on his lap. His round ears were flushed, and his trim athletic figure slouched slightly as he spoke with the undertone of pre-wed lust.

"What's gotten into you, handsome? It's like you're nineteen again and we just met." He had Lydia giggling. The stewardess put a hand on his shoulder, asking him to turn off his electronic device, and Sam had to pull out of the call. All he wanted was to smell her. And taste. There were things a man could do that only got better with age, but he wouldn't have his chance tonight.

Sam sighed and took off his jacket, settling in for the flight. It was then that he noticed the Japanese-marked letter sticking out from an interior pocket. Mrs. B. must have slipped it in.

Lexington, Kentucky

Parker Beam picked up Samuel Dugranval in a 1977 Pontiac Firebird. Red, with an aggressive grille, quad square headlamps, gold-billet wheels, a 6.6-liter engine—it was the ultimate muscle car, complete with Mastercraft Avenger G/T tires. An impressive ride, even for a Kentucky aristocrat like Beam.

"Good to see you, my old friend," Parker bellowed, lanky and leaning against the hood. "Nice suit."

It was a balmy seventy-two degrees at the Lexington strip, and Samuel was wearing a slim-cut, bespoke number made by a tucked-away tailor in Hong Kong. "*What* a beauty, Parker," Sam said, looking at the machine, then looking at the sky. "And it's perfect weather for a drive."

The two hugged and got into the car. They exited past iron-sculpted thoroughbreds, with a bit of showmanship, showing off, and gravel spinning under the tires. There was an unspoken excitement between them, an electricity in the air about what Samuel may have just discovered in the Yankee territories of upstate New York.

The sun was going down, and the smell of horse manure, grass shavings, and fertile Kentucky soil came up. Through the rolling pastures of the horse-breeding estates, beneath a reddening sky, Samuel watched the sun, far and aged, sink into the horizon—red sky through red oak, chestnut oak, black oak, Ohio buckeye, yellow buckeye, pignut, walnut, sycamore, birch, sugar maple, *so many trees*, magnolia, hawthorn, *and so fast*, black cherry, redbud even redder in this light, and white oak; the very white oak of bourbon casks.

Kentucky. Land of vice, Mecca of horse betting, bourbon drinking, and burly tobacco. Home to pitch-happy farmers, Arabian sires, chic sheiks and their private jets, an estate of the Queen of England, and Farrah Fawcett's widower's castle. See, Washington never reached western Pennsylvania. Instead he allowed his troops to go on ahead (the Scottish-Irish farmers disbanded when they heard how many showed up to fight). Washington, instead, turned back for Philadelphia, having demonstrated the Federal power. But what did Federal power matter to the then Wild West? Pennsylvania had been tamed, but the unbridled spirit of the American frontier was already placing its bets on Kentucky. Many of the Scottish-Irish settlers moved on over the Alleghany Mountains, down into a once forbidden land that had been the stomping grounds of Daniel Boone, Jessie James, his brothers and gang—a land of corn and wood, limestone water, and four distinct seasons of weather.

Driving along these Kentucky roads, Sam felt camaraderie with those of Washington's troops who rode to quell the rebellion but did not return home—the soldiers who fled the army and rode south for Kentucky as well. With the goal of expanding the western border of the United States, Jefferson had made the offer of four hundred free acres to any man willing to grow corn and build a cabin in Kentucky, and these homesteads were far enough from Philadelphia that dodging tax was practically a given. It was whiskey heaven, and from this heaven came what would be known as bourbon.

"You know Jeffer—," Sam said, but Parker pulled the emergency brake before he could finish, sliding into a gravel driveway.

"Linda hates it when I do that," Beam beamed.

The home of the Heaven Hill Master Distiller was a red-brick colonial with a chimney up either side. The grand columned porch was set up with teakwood chairs. They pulled in, and Linda Beam came to the screen door, all smiles, silk, and charm. A hound lay in the early dark upon the cool floor of the porch, getting up to bay and nip at the knees of the men.

Samuel's head was embraced by Linda's hospitable chest. She had not seen him since he had been poisoned earlier that year. "Oh, Sam, we were so frightened for you."

"Don't remind him," said Parker. "Let the man inside for a drink."

The hound bayed and threw up. "Don't mind the dog," Parker said and shooed the animal away from the mess. Sam stepped to the side. "He does that. He likes to eat the compost. It's a hassle, but the green movement, you know. Green movement, my foot. We've always been green. Every hand in Kentucky washes the other. Bourbon has never used additives, we give our slop at the distillery to livestock, and we ship our old barrels to Scotland for reuse. We don't need no tree-huggin' activists to tell us what's right."

Linda rolled her eyes and pushed the men into the kitchen, where they were met face-on by a life-sized bust of a horse.

"That's new," said Sam.

Parker went to sideboard and began to mix the cocktails.

"I'll take one of those," said Rob Hutchins, US brand ambassador for Heaven Hill, who had just let himself in the house. "Already made you one," Parker said, giving the drinks a quick stir before they all sat down. Linda had prepared a beautiful Bibb salad, cheesy grits, and a generous cut of local rib eye. Though Sam had already eaten on the plane, this was a spread he could not resist.

"Dugranval, it's good to see you," Hutchins said, "Last I heard, you got poisoned."

Parker started laughing, revealing a mouthful of greens. "You didn't lose your sense of the tactile did you, Sam-yull?" Parker teased Sam about his phobia of losing the passions in his life: smell, sight, taste, touch, sound. What else was there? *Try to love without the senses...*

When Samuel was sixteen, he had suffered a grade-three concussion. He was kicked in the face at a championship Muay Thai fight in Paris against an opponent from Hat Yai, Thailand. He lost consciousness, lost the fight, and woke up having lost 95 percent of his olfactory functioning. It took him nearly a year to recover, and intensive training at a perfume institute in Grasse to regain and better his nose. And though he graduated with honors, the psychological damage haunted him still.

Parker loved to give him shit. "Quit hiking down memory lane alone."

"Yes, I was poisoned," Sam said to Rob. "I almost went blind."

"You sure it wasn't from jerkin' off, eh?" Rob said, nearly choking on a bite.

Parker showed his big fake teeth, a smiling replica of the horse above.

CHAPTER FIVE

"**I** have only expelled one student in the history of IFDM," Sam told the table, sipping on his second cocktail, "and it nearly cost me my life. Tado Ehime Koga—better known by his classmates as The Sulfur. The kid was rotten. Last May, he sent me a bottle of quince brandy with a note: 'I'm still trying. I hope this is to your taste. Sincerely, Tado.' That little prick."

It was an obsession with quince: Samuel's soft spot from his tree-house days in Burgundy, autumn in the orchards harvesting the fruit for his mother's quince pies. Perhaps nostalgia had 'blinded' his nose. Perhaps not.

"I was an idiot," Sam went on. "The brandy was loaded with methanol, and I couldn't smell it. We analyzed it in the lab after the fact. So did the court, and although they found him liable, their verdict was that it was not malicious." Samuel scoffed. "But the aptitude of that synthetic mask…no one can 'accidentally' produce a mask so sophisticated that I can't pick it up on the nose. We tried to pull in my old professor from Grasse to testify to that extent, but the defense wouldn't let us, said it was speculative."

Parker shook his head knowingly, cutting into his rib eye.

Sam took another sip. "I had brought the bottle with me to IFDM's annual Alumni Dinner at Daniel's after sampling a full glass earlier that day. I gave quite a heart-warming speech, if I may say so, about how proud I was of all my graduates, then I made a complete fool out of myself. I announced that I had no failures and presented Koga's bottle. I told everyone that he might have cleaned up his act and invited them to have *un doigt*, a taste."

Rob chuckled.

Sam ignored him. "When the bottle came around to me, I was overly excited and poured a deep glass. You know, in my opinion, it's the cutting of the heads and tails from the heart of the distillate that separates amateurs from the real artists. I had high hopes. The distillation of brandy is especially tricky in this regard due to the level of pectin in certain fruits. And Koga knew this—especially considering that he chose quince, which is inherently high in pectin and can get dangerous."

"You really think we need a lecture on heads and tails?" Parker interjected.

"How much did you drink?" Linda gasped.

"Well, I had one glass at about 2:00 p.m., well before the dinner, and another glass and a half after the meal. I'm a sucker for quince. It seemed to be a diligent balance of fruits and honey, a little peppery at the end, with a long, pronounced—"

"A long and pronounced finish all the way to the emergency room," Parker broke in. He'd heard the story before.

"We stayed late at the restaurant, and when I stood to leave, I could tell something was wrong. I was drunk, *really* drunk, and my vision was starting to blur. I was all confused. At first I thought it was the cocktails followed by wine followed by brandy. Normally I don't mix, see, but we knew the alumni would want cocktails, so I had the bartender serve *real* Manhattans. The old kind. Washington's recipe of small beer, rum, and sugar."

"Speakin' of cocktails…" Parker jumped up and grabbed the empty glasses from the table. He disappeared into the kitchen.

Sam turned to Rob and Linda. "You know, Manhattan comes from the Delaware Indian tribe's 'Manahactanienk,' which means 'island of general intoxication.' Even way back then, New York City was a place of lustful thirsts, shameless behavior, and hallucinations." Sam put his napkin on his plate. "And stepping out onto the curb that night, I felt I was stepping into my own private island of hell."

"Jesus, you're some storyteller," Rob broke in. "Frenchy, you should sit around a campfire with some real Kentucky folk." No one laughed. Parker returned with fresh drinks and pulled his chair closer to Linda's, the two listening on with Southern compassion, genuine but a tad performed.

"By the time I managed to fall into a cab, I was nearly blind. I was running my hands all over the vinyl, and I couldn't tell if I was uptown, downtown, or in Cincinnati. The driver took me to the Presbyterian Hospital where they shot me up with a heavy dose of ethanol to inhibit the methanol, and within a few days, I was watching movies with my wife. So you see, Robert?" Sam gave the brand ambassador a surprisingly clear-eyed stare. "It was corn that save my life."

"And the alumni? Did anyone else at the dinner get sick?" Linda asked.

"Sadly, yes. Quite a number of them had a rough night, but I was the only one hospitalized."

Linda stood, gave Sam a pat on the arm, then deftly pulled the dinner plates. She went to the kitchen, and Parker followed, pinching at her tail. Sam and Rob sat in awkward silence for a moment until Parker returned with fresh glasses and the bottle of Evan Williams. He poured four straight bourbons, and Linda returned with a steaming bourbon pecan pie and homemade vanilla bean ice cream.

"Now, Sam," Parker said, "I want to hear more about this whiskey you sampled in upstate New York."

The next morning, Sam woke up late. He hated that. His head hurt, and he was still wearing his suit. The night had ended in a blur. Sam vaguely remembered finishing off the bottle of bourbon, Parker telling dirty jokes, and Rob mumbling something about catching a plane to Vegas in the morning. *God, I hope Rob didn't drive.*

The house was quiet. Samuel took a cold shower, changed into fresh clothes, took his knife out of his luggage and tucked it in his pocket, then came down from the guest quarters into the kitchen. Waiting for him on the counter was a piece of Kentucky coffee cake.

He groggily looked up at the horse and asked, "Where is everyone?" Scanning for the coffee pot, he took a bite of the cake, and noticed the keys to the Firebird sitting atop a note:

"Something horrible has happened. We're at the Bardstown office.—Linda"

CHAPTER SIX

"**W**oodrow Campbell is dead," Parker said. "Murdered. They found his body at Four Roses early this morning."

"What? Woody?" Sam looked into Parker's bone-tired face. They were in a spare room at Heaven Hill's corporate office; Linda's arms were around Parker's neck, her cheek on his head. The leaf pattern on the floor seemed suddenly garish with its sheen of spill-proof polypropylene, and a vibrating wave of blackness seized Samuel's guts. Linda, he noticed, was wearing the same sweater she had on the night before.

Samuel looked out the window. "Murdered?" The world turned alien, turned against him, his own mortality now a shrill and omnipresent alarm. Sam thought about Woodrow Campbell's son and grandchildren. He thought about his own son, Leo, and his wife, Lydia. They could be taken from him at any moment. Or he from them. "Who would kill such a brilliant man?" Samuel took several steps back, suddenly not knowing where to stand.

Parker didn't reply—he just stared into his hands.

Sam had seen Campbell only a few months back, exultant and full of ideas. Campbell had just returned from a trip to Japan where he was working as a consultant for Suntory, and he and Sam had talked for hours about the future of distillation over dinner in New York.

The phone on Parker's desk rang. They all stared at it, frozen. Parker finally answered. "Of course, Nate, I'll be right there." Nathaniel was Woodrow Campbell's son.

"Sam-yull," Parker said, "will you drive me to Four Roses? It doesn't make sense. They found his body in the fermentation room... Woody's...Woody's body. Nate wants me to come over to make sure the cops don't screw anything up."

Why was Campbell in the fermentation room at Four Roses—a distillery owned by Kirin, the direct competitor of his employer, Suntory? "Of course, Parker," Sam said, forcing down the thick lump in his throat and putting a hand into his pocket for the keys.

They took the back roads to Lawrenceburg, heading out past white rickhouses stained black with torula—the harmless fungus that feeds off the evaporating bourbon from the barrels known to the tourists as the "angel's share." They wrapped around north and out of town on Route 62 toward Bloomfield, the distillery pup, Lucky, chasing them to the property line.

They drove by a farm equipment shop directly across from a sign for a limousine service. They passed American-Fuji Bottling Corp., and the local high school with a sign that read "Nelson County vs. Bardstown, double header chili supper." They came upon a line of spruce trees and drove through a cluster of World-War-II-era single-family homes. The land rolled and began to open up. They passed a trailer with a spring horse in the yard for a kid to ride, a black board fence, an old tobacco barn, and an abandoned brick house with a broad-winged hawk perched on its roof.

A dark cat walked down a gravel path. There was a black barn with a new tin roof. They passed "Judy's Hair and Electronics," and a farm with black cows standing in a field. A few willows, a maple, hickory. An irrigation ditch followed the road.

They headed east into the town of Bloomfield and into the Marathon gas station where Parker gassed up the Firebird, and Samuel went inside to find a cup of coffee—he was desperate to escape this dream. The wind through the canopy over the pumps made a shrieking sound, like the cries of river gulls, and perched on a rack just inside the filling station door was *The Kentucky Standard*, the local rag.

Barrels of Blood (Murder) at Four Roses Distillery

Lawrenceburg, KY—The body of local whiskey legend, Woodrow Campbell, was discovered at 5:00 a.m. this morning in the back of the fermentation room at Four Roses Distillery on Bonds Mill Road.

The security guard who found the body was unavailable for comment and is being treated for shock.

Anderson County coroner, Brian Ritchie, said the cause of death was "loss of blood as a result of multiple stab wounds, dismemberment, and mutilation."

Anderson County Sheriff, Troy Young, was available for a statement. "This appears to be a killing involving a sword or knife attack," said Young, adding that he and his officers will investigate local as well as international suspects based on all evidence and possible motives. So far, no suspects have been taken into custody, but already there are rumors of Japanese involvement due to Campell's recent business dealings with the Japanese distiller, Suntory, and the buyout of the local Four Roses distillery by one of Suntory's competitors, Kirin. Over the past months, there have been rising tensions between locals in the bourbon industry and the recent influx of Japanese business owners, and some speculators think Campbell was a victim of this animosity. "The murder weapon appears to be a long knife with a blade approximately the length of a samurai sword," Young said.

Woodrow Campbell was a grain chemist and master distiller who was best known as an innovator of groundbreaking whiskies in the global market. He spent nearly four decades at Brown-Forman, one of the largest American-owned wine and spirits companies, before going out on his own as a consultant for various global corporations, mainly Suntory. He loved horse races and always invited a crowd to sit in his suite at the Derby.

Woodrow is survived by his wife, Beitris, son, Nathaniel, and three grandchildren.

Samuel threw the paper back onto the rack and dialed New York. "David, listen to me. Kentucky's a mess. Woodrow Campbell has been murdered and the local paper is jumping to dangerous conclusions."

"Sam? What? Where are—"

"Parker's in a bad state. We're driving right into what I'm sure is going to be a media frenzy."

"What are you talking about? Campbell? *The* Woodrow Campbell?"

"And I haven't even started to look at Parker's research. I'm on my way to the murder scene now. David, get on the next flight. I need you here."

Parker was waiting in the car for Sam with his head leaned against the passenger window. Sam got in without a word and pulled out of the station onto 555 toward Springfield and the Bluegrass Parkway. A procession of tobacco trucks hauling trailers full of harvested tobacco plants pulled out in front of them, the tobacco stalks hanging upside down from wooden drying pegs, thick and densely packed. The undersides of the leaves were slightly yellowed from the dry fall, and the thicker green leaves below flocked the wheel wells, the painted trailers, and the gates.

"Marlboro Lights," said Parker. "Those are Larry Calvert's trucks."

They passed a Dollar General, a union hall, then a red and white striped barn with glass-less dormers. There was an open, empty mailbox hanging sideways on a fence, trees cut away from power lines, and workhorses feeding. They came upon an unwalled cemetery that spanned the road with crooked lines of small headstones. Above them, on a hill, rose an impressive red tobacco barn with an American flag flying over its black roof. The ground level of the barn was open-air, allowing tobacco to dry.

The tobacco truck in front of them turned left up to the barn. "Yup, Larry Calvert is a good old boy," said Parker "He went to church with my son before Craig and his ex-wife split up. Everyone's been talkin' about that barn; it's the biggest one in the area. Enough tobacco dryin' up in there to keep New York smokin' for a day or two."

Samuel laughed, desperate for relief. "So this is Phillip Morris country? I never thought about that. I assumed they got their tobacco in Virginia."

"Burly is a lighter tobacco," Parker replied, "and since 80 percent of United States Burly is out of Kentucky, a lot of the lighter cigarettes source tobacco from here. A lot is also shipped out as filler to the Chinese." Parker then went quiet and looked out the window.

Samuel turned up the volume on the stereo. The sweet and synco-pated voice of Carmen McRae sang a ballad of a lover gone: a song full of questions and loss. Each man turned inward.

Samuel thought about Woody. Apart from David, Woodrow Campbell was the person with whom Samuel had wanted to share his discovery of Barclay's unearthed bourbon the most. A few weeks after their dinner in New York, Sam had joined Woody at small late-summer horse race outside of Lexington. Woody had just released Paradise Creek—his latest product that he had developed with his son. Instead of talking about his new product, Woody had fervently deconstructed the mash bills of various Japanese and American whiskies, barely watch-ing the track. Sam remembered him in his white seersucker sports coat and his signature round-rimmed glasses going on and on about the unparalleled meticulousness and innovation of the Japanese—and the wealth of opportunity in appropriating Japanese techniques for bourbon.

Could this man really be dead? Everyone loved him, and as fierce as the Japanese could be, was it really in keeping with their mentality to slaughter a proponent of their craftsmanship with a samurai sword? It's too unreal. And what could Campbell possibly be doing in Kirin's fermentation room? Samuel's heart stiffened, a determination to find the killer pressing upon the anguish in his chest.

"Parker, there's going to be a bunch of local cops, and my guess is that the FBI will be taking over soon. I didn't want to tell you, but the papers are rumoring Japanese foul play. What tasteless crap. Whatever statement you put out through the Heaven Hill PR department, keep it short. Craig has everything under control in Louisville today?"

Parker gave a nod.

"Good. There's going to be a lot of questions for us. We'll have our hands tied." Sam's voice lowered, lost its strength. "And, Parker, did Woody have enemies?"

Parker shook his head no.

The Firebird passed the original, but now abandoned, office of Four Roses, a basic four-walled, white cement building that looked like a jailhouse from the old American West. They crossed a small bridge over a sudsy waterfall and were hit with the overwhelming scent of fermentation slop.

"Something's off," said Sam. "They normally don't have that much slop. And look, no steam. This can't be good."

CHAPTER SEVEN

Police cruisers crammed the lot. Some were double and triple parked, their revolving lights dim in the daylight. Samuel guessed that most of the Anderson County Police force had reported to the scene. "Jesus," he said.

Sam pulled the Firebird beside the visitor's center, a Spanish mission-style building with a barrel swing out front and a Kentucky flag flying at half-mast. Two cops stood near the entrance, and one of them gave Parker a familiar yet solemn hello as he and Sam walked in.

The gift shop was dark. A collapsible table in the hallway held several pots of dark coffee, cream, and bear claws, which complimented the sweet smell coming from a display barrel of twenty-one-year-old Four Roses Bourbon. Samuel put his nose near the bunghole for a whiff before entering the main room, where policemen sat in clumps of chairs and Woodrow's widow stood alone by the far wall.

Beitris Campbell had her arms across her chest. Her hands were gripping her sides, and her breath was shallow. In one hand, she held a crumpled wet napkin. When she saw Parker, she let out a low moan. She collapsed into him as he hugged her.

"Oh, Parker," she sobbed. "Oh, thank God you're here."

A few cops stood, but did not approach. Samuel looked through the glass of the side door to the distillery where more policemen were gathered. Red tape ran across the back door, though it remained ajar.

Nathaniel Campbell came in, grabbed Parker's shoulder and rubbed his mother's back. "Thanks for comin'. It's a shit show here," he said, his face expressionless, his body stiff with shock. "We've been here since 6:00 a.m. and still don't know anything. The cops have shut down production. They won't let us in the fermentation room, and they're draining the tanks. Dad would hate this."

Beitris sobbed harder, gasping multiple times, trying to breathe. Parker took her over to a chair. Her hand rose and fell upon her chest beneath a thin camisole, the skin on her clavicle red from crying. She drew the sweater closed, a futile act of composure, her light eyes and cheeks also rosy with distress.

Nathaniel, as if in order to not break down himself, turned his attention to Sam. "I didn't know you were in town."

"Just got in last night. I'm really sorry, Nate. I loved your father."

Nathaniel nodded. "Well, let's get over there and see about gettin' past that red tape. I need to have a look."

Sam firmly grabbed his arm. "I'll look for you," he said. "Nate, there are things a son shouldn't see."

CHAPTER EIGHT

The emblem looked bloody. Four crimson roses, thickly painted, each as large as Samuel himself, were emblazoned on the distillery's far wall. One rose reached up into the peak of the A-frame, bright under the skylights, and the other three were in shadow below. There was death in the smell of fermentation in the air.

The open fermentation tanks were in various stages of being evacuated, and a loud sucking noise shook the floorboards. Each red cypress tank could hold almost 16,500 gallons of mash, though each was at a different stage of being drained. The steel beer well, which fed into the copper still, was empty. An old ladder with sharp hooks to latch onto the tanks leaned against the rear wall, and a mirage gleamed over the liquid that had yet to be drained—a heat wave effect of the yeast converting sugar to alcohol. The surface of the mash in the younger tanks foamed with large yellow bubbles.

Each tank was four hours apart from the next in the fermentation process, and Sam knew each tank was cleaned every seventy-two hours, but never all at once. *Never like this.* The monetary value alone of what was being sucked out of the room was staggering.

Someone put a hand on Sam's shoulder. "Do you belong here?"

Sam turned around.

A policeman stood, one hand on his holster, the other firmly gripping Sam's shirt. He looked like a kid.

"Who ordered these vats to be drained?" Sam asked. "Do you know how many barrels of mash you've wasted, not to mention the production that is on halt? I represent the Institute of Fermentation,

Distillation, and Maturation in New York. The family of the deceased sent me here to make sure things are done right."

The cop looked unsure of what to say. He was young—a local, corn-fed cop with a baby face and a fledgling mustache.

"Where was the body?" Sam asked.

"Over there in the other room, by the exit, next to vat twenty," replied the kid, and let go of his grip.

Samuel started heading toward the back.

"Don't touch anything," the cop said and followed him in.

Samuel walked over to vat twenty, which was half full, its contents slowly draining. His stomach lurched. The floor in front of him was covered in blood. It looked like the entire body had been emptied right there. An incomprehensible chalk outline was marked out. *Which lines represent Woody's arms? Which his legs?* Samuel watched his step and inched closer to where the body had been. He squatted and saw that blood had leaked through the cracks of the floorboards, staining the concrete one story below. Samuel's insides quivered like the air above the tanks.

A steel door banged, followed by sharp, metallic footsteps.

"OK, that's enough," the kid cop said. Sam stood, and the two stepped through one of the archways that split the back of the fermentation room from the front. A darkly suited man looked down upon them from the elevator deck, leaning on the copper railing. A net hung below him, level to the floor of the deck and out over the first vats, to keep Bourbon Trail tourists from dropping anything into the mash. But this man didn't look like the type to drop the sunglasses he wore. Samuel knew exactly *what* this man was.

"What are you two doing down there?" the man asked. He wore a thin tie.

The Feds, Samuel thought, and let out a low groan. "Here we go."

The kid looked confused and then indignant. "I'm Anderson County PD."

"He was just escorting me out—" Samuel started to explain.

"Who are you?" the man interrupted.

"I am a friend of Woody's."

"Friend or no friend, everyone's a suspect." From where the man in the tie stood, the world was composed of symmetrically intersecting bars and support beams, each painted green to match the emblem of the roses' leaves. The man perfunctorily walked down the stairs and demanded Samuel's ID.

"I know your face," the Fed said as he got closer to Sam. "You run that distillation school in New York."

"That's right," Sam said, locking eyes with the agent.

"You're contaminating the crime scene, trespassing, and interfering with a federal investigation. Let's take this show outside. Anderson County, you stay here and do your job. No one is allowed through these doors but me and my forensics team."

They walked out of the fermentation room, over a metal walkway, the Fed closely following Sam. To their left was a two-story column still, and in front of them was the large copper pot still, with a sign labeling it "The Doubler." The air, which normally smelled like yeast, was astringent.

"What are you doing down here, Dugranval? Why are you in this state?"

"What do you know about this murder, so far?" Sam asked, ignoring the question. "You guys are smart enough, I assume, to know you can't dust for prints with all the visitors that come through this place, so you're draining the tanks? What do you think you're going to find at the bottom of those vats? A note?"

"We're checking for poison, among other things. It's standard procedure."

"Well, those slop tanks go into a cooling house, and then to feed cattle. If the local cows drop dead, we'll know it wasn't the locals out cow tipping. What's your name, agent?"

"I am Federal Agent Randall Lefevre. And like I said, you're a suspect. Don't leave this county until you hear from my lips otherwise."

31

Sam slammed the distillery door behind him, leaving the agent inside. National news vans had arrived, and satellite towers were being erected in the private lot behind the Four Roses visitor's center and corporate offices. Several large touring coaches and a mobile home indicated more FBI presence.

A team of men and women in white plastic suits huddled around the taped-off exit at the back of the fermentation room. They wore blue gloves, yellow boots, and black plastic kneepads, which were sewn into their pants. Some carried nets and tubes, others hooks. Sam watched them for a few minutes, trying to see what they were up to, but he was too far away to get a good look. He gave up and went to look for Nate.

The visitor's center was twice as full as when Sam had left it. The entire bourbon community and the entire Kentucky news force seemed to be packed in, and Sam felt as if he were running out of air. The light was on in the gift shop, and even it was swarmed cops and reporters who were manhandling souvenirs. Samuel scanned for signs of Nathaniel, Beatris, and Parker, but they were nowhere to be found. He pulled out his phone.

"We had to get out of there," said Parker over the line. "We're headed to the Huddle House for some pancakes. Nate and Beitris haven't eaten today, and I thought I might make 'em try." Sam was relieved; he didn't want Beitris to have to deal with the media. Also he had no idea what to say to Nathaniel. He hung up and called David. The call went straight to voicemail. "David, call me when you hit Lexington."

A newscaster started talking behind him, and Samuel began to plug his ear but stopped.

"Breaking news from the Four Roses Distillery in Lawrenceburg. The FBI has found a knife, assumed to be the murder weapon, in fermenter twenty—next to where the body of local distiller, Woodrow Campbell, was discovered earlier this morning. No specifics on the weapon have been released, but the president of Four Roses and his assistant, both Japanese management from Kirin, were brought in to translate Japanese script that was printed on the knife's blade. There will be more from WAVE 3 News on this startling development as further information is released. This is Dawne Gee reporting live from Four Roses."

Why would the killer throw the knife into a fermenter? thought Sam. *Everyone knows those vats are hand-cleaned every three days.*

"Maybe the killer was in a hurry," said Agent Lefevre, like a mind reader, walking up behind Sam.

CHAPTER NINE

It felt good to let the Firebird open up. Samuel took the back roads toward the Man O' War Airport in Lexington, hugging the curves and rolls of the Kentucky hills. It felt good to get away from Four Roses, the pressure, those cops, and to have some time alone. The world was fast alongside him, then gone. There was only new road ahead.

Maybe he would take David to the Kentucky Speedway before this trip was up. David would love that. Sam was tearing hell through the roads, assaulting his grief with wind, testing what Parker's Firebird could really do. He thought about how moonrunners must have felt back in the years of prohibition, shooting around these same curves. Souped-up cars with two-hundred-gallon moonshine tanks, modified coupes with impeccable maneuvering, backseats full of bottles—those rural boys getting top dollar by breaking the law at breakneck speeds.

Sam was too old to be a moonrunner, he knew, but he imagined himself in that era, working a copper still like the father of legendary Junior Jones. He would feed fires with his hands, run the whole process by touch, by nose, by temperature and time. A sensualist's life lived fully for the sake of whiskey and freedom. The younger men could have their thrills on midnight runs while he cooked alone under the cover of oak and spruce.

With moonshine money and mechanical know-how, boys like Junior Jones and his brothers had built the fastest rides ever known. They did away with the rear and passenger seats to make more room for the illicit booze, added serious suspensions to handle the extra weight, and slapped steel plates on the radiators to strengthen the frame and support the load. They would pack up their buggies and fly the bootlegger's trail, more often than not being chased full-way by the cops. This was the inception of the stock car, which, in turn, spawned NASCAR. Jones was one of the nation's first famous racecar drivers. In fact, nearly all early race drivers were involved in running hooch.

After prohibition, the boys needed a reason to keep their cars tuned, as there was an endless audience for the racing sport. *If prohibition had never ended,* thought Sam, *imagine the caliber of vehicle that would be running 'shine now! To have boys reaching those speeds on these passenger roads...*He got goose bumps at the thought. But there were real concerns, his boy and wife in Manhattan. Woody was dead, and he needed something concrete to say to Nathaniel.

Sam passed a car and cut back into his lane as fast as he had ever driven. The wheel felt different at this speed. Harder. He shifted. *A man has only the comfort of violent power to protect him, or of goodness—toward women and men younger than himself. Of course there are other comforts: the sensual world, knowledge, and craft,* but when Sam considered himself, driving too fast, gunning it toward Lexington past the big-money horse estates, he saw a man who had seen a brutal engine under the hood of life.

David, in some sense oblivious, was about to step out of the sky into Kentucky's autumn sunshine. But take a man and blind him, place him crawling in the backseat of a cab in New York City, give him a son and a wife to care for, let him see there is something or someone out there willing to kill him or his family and friends, and soon enough, that man begins to see what lies beneath the civilities of daily life.

Sam knew this, and now Nathaniel did too. From the moment Nate answered that predawn phone call from the police, he knew and felt more than Sam could ever imagine. Sam's stomach turned, and he shifted down, seeing the airport turn-off ahead. *There were boys who died in those cars running 'shine.* Sam saw a broad-winged hawk perched on a length of board fencing. *Woody's body drained onto that floor.* He saw two forearms leading toward the wheel. Sam thought of how lucky anyone is to be behind the controls of a fast machine, alone for a while. But something was chasing him down. He had things to figure out. Sam turned into the airport and parked, stepped out of the car and walked to the fence where David's plane was touching down. Samuel's face was wet with wind and tears.

CHAPTER TEN

David was all eyes on the Firebird. Samuel handed him the keys, and David lit up with anticipation. There was a moment of doubt in David's expression, as if the keys might be taken back, but he did not wait to find out. He climbed in, pushed the seat back, and turned the starter. The sound was startling.

"Careful, David. This is Parker's baby."

David drove the route Sam instructed, dragging the Firebird from stop light to stop light. They passed that prodigal castle where Farrah Fawcett's widower rented out rooms for a thousand dollars a night—to Arabs, mostly, or so Sam had heard. Stop and gun under the sunshine, they passed Huddle Houses, big-box stores, the Bluegrass Community and Technical College, and a hand-stenciled sign that read, "Pro wrestling every Sunday at the Eagle Lake Convention Center."

David gave Sam a look. "Pro wrestling? We have see *that*." They caught a string of green fields and turned onto a back road. David finally let the engine out, hitting fifth gear and grinning wide. Sam threatened to take David's driving privileges away, but couldn't help but smile himself.

The two reached Bardstown and pulled up in front of the Old Talbott Tavern and Inn. "They say this place is full of ghosts," Samuel said. "And each room is named for a famous hero in Kentucky's history, something you'd appreciate, so I thought we'd stay here." The inn had been there since 1769—the date engraved in its marble front step. A brochure in the lobby said it was the oldest western stagecoach stop in America—a place where all types of itinerants and explorers passed through.

"Around the time of the French Revolution," Samuel read on, "the exiled French King Louis Philippe and his entourage stayed here. To cope with their homesickness for France, they painted elaborate murals of the gardens of Versailles. Later, when Jesse James and his gang moved in, they would get drunk upstairs and shoot at the painted birds in the trees. Bullet holes are still lodged in the walls."

"I'd love to have lived back then," David said. He was a huge fan of Jesse James, Daniel Boone, and all the outlaws of the West.

They took David's duffel bag inside, where a busty woman in a teal sweat suit dangled keys as if she'd been dangling them all day. She made a production of telling them about the inn, recounting stories about ghosts like scandalous gossip. As she talked, she smacked her gum and fidgeted with her thin-rimmed spectacles—it seemed she was the type of woman David would resist hitting on. But he hit on her anyway. Samuel chuckled and blew air out of his nose.

In the end, Samuel booked the Lincoln Suite for himself—Old Abe having been born and raised in Kentucky. David, however, was not able to get the Daniel Boone room, or the Jesse James Room (under renovation), and had to settle for the Anton Heinrich Room—a tiny space named after a Bohemian violinist he'd never heard of.

The woman chewing gum took them upstairs to a large vestibule with a fireplace and a few chairs, onto which several of the larger guest rooms opened up, including Sam's. David's room was down a narrow hall. "The Heinrich room is the most active," she said, eying David and tapping her long boney fingers with dark red nails on the sign beside his door. "The ghost of an old man lives in here." She opened the door to a room suffocating in floral wallpaper. "That stuffed chair is where he likes to sit. He also likes to wake guests up in the night and ask them where Shelby went," she watched David's reaction closely. "If you leave anything on that chair, the next morning you might just find it flung across the room. And I definitely wouldn't sit in it if I were you."

David shook his arm like he was trying to bring his sleeve down, as if adjusting his cuff. The motion made no sense, and the woman laughed.

They went back downstairs to the front desk. David ate a stale bourbon caramel that was on display by the register, and paid thirty-five cents for it. Samuel paid for the rooms. Then he and David went out across the street to a greasy joint with a big black sign that read "The Stable." It was an old barn that had been converted into a pub. Inside, paintings of sports figures in primary colors hung on the walls beside lids of bourbon casks signed by master distillers. Miniature stock cars lined the backside of the bar. The two saddled up, ordered burgers and beer, and Sam filled David in on the scene at Four Roses and his run-in with Agent Lefevre.

"That bastard called me a suspect," Samuel said, sipping his beer.

"That's absurd. Anyone who knows anything knows how close you and Campbell were." David took a big gulp of brew and gave Samuel an encouraging nod.

"Forget him," Samuel scoffed. "The point is you are here now, thank God. And if we can't help Campbell, the least we can do is figure out where Barclay's bourbon came from."

"I ran a chemical analysis of what was left in the syringe," David said becoming excited.

"You have the print out?"

"Of course." David reached into his back pocket and pulled out several folded sheets of paper. "By the way, how does my hair look?" he asked, giving an impish wink. "The smell is starting to wash out, right?" He took a swig of beer and grinned. He knew he had Sam's attention. "I was nervous at first that the damage would be permanent," he laughed. "But look at it now—"

"David! Don't make me hurt your pretty face. Let's see the numbers."

"And what do I get in return?" David said raising an eyebrow and dabbing a fry in a swamp of ketchup and mayo. "You know I switched barbers. I used to go to this old Jewish guy in Morningside Heights; you know the place, right? But I got so tired of him always talking about himself and how we're all going to die in the end, hair all over the floor. Well, and his hands shook. So I found this place. The guy's a dandy, and he does a pretty good job, don't you think? And he's the same price as…"

"*David!*" Sam broke into a smile.

"All right, all right. Here."

Sam grabbed the creased pages and spread them out onto the bar.

"See this?" David asked, pointing to numbers he had circled in red. "The starch ratio is extremely high."

Sam looked at the numbers, then looked at David. "This stuff is the real thing," he said. "This whiskey must have been made with some aboriginal strain of corn, back before cross-breeding made American cobs huge and loaded with sugar." Sam took the final sip from his beer and stared into the bottom of the glass.

"I have an old college buddy who works down here, a corn chemist," David said. "Maybe I could—"

"First I want you to get over to the Oscar Getz Museum," Sam broke in. "See what you can find out about native strains of corn. Remember: we're looking for old, small stuff. I'm going to drive out to ZAK cooperage. I have some business to tend to there." He stood. "Let's get the check."

David set out on foot. It felt good to walk, as he had been cramped all afternoon on the plane. The streets of Bardstown looked recently repaved, but the buildings showed their years. Just off Foster Avenue, there was a large Catholic church named for Saint Joseph, with a statue of the saint out front, arms stretched forth. Another church stood a few blocks away with imposing stained glass windows and a tall white spire, which was not used as a point of triangulation for mapping, David figured, as he did not find a metal plate anywhere on the grounds. But there were many towers in this area that were used as points of reference in the early days of America. That he knew.

Bardstown was similar to the towns one found up in New England, small quotidian villages with stone structures and storefront-downtowns where businesses thrived. Aside from places like the Stable or the Old Talbott Inn and its neighbor, the Jailer's Inn (which had more Western appeal), this had the charm of New England north of New York City. But something was different about Kentucky that was harder to put a finger on. David sensed something claustrophobic to the terrain. It wasn't just the reserved quality of New England, but a sort of a suspicion that lurked behind the more Southern attributes of hospitality. The sky in Kentucky felt low too. Kentucky seemed a place of clans, where one was meant to be in relationship with one's kin only or with a few other families, but not many more. Outsiders did not seem welcome here.

CHAPTER ELEVEN

The Oscar Getz Museum of Whiskey History was housed in a stately three-story brick colonial set back from the street by a manicured lawn. The maples in front were just beginning to turn with the season, and David walked under them with the upward gaze of a tourist, and the resolute strides of a New Yorker getting back to his country roots. He accidentally opened both doors going in, and he would have been embarrassed by his grand entrance had he not been met by only a silent hall. It seemed as if no one was around.

David coughed. An ornate ironwork sign bearing the name of the museum hung over his head, and before him, display cases ran the length of a short hall. Unsure of where to start or what he was looking for exactly, David took the exhibits in the order that they caught his eye. He walked over to a case of old square-shouldered bottles, one with a big sheriff's star in the center of its label. "Belle of Anderson," it read, "Bottled in Bond—For Medicinal Use Only." Next to that was a bottle of Old Crow marked spring of 1925. Old Stagg, Old Briargate, Echo Springs, Belle of Nelson, Tom Moore—they sounded like places and characters from folktales, not bottles of hooch. David scanned the exhibit notes: "medicinal whiskies provided to the lame and blind during Prohibition after the passage of the Volstead Act in 1919." Good old American ingenuity.

He moved on, passing two jars full of poplar plugs and cedar wedges used to stop barrel leaks, and paused in front of a display of arrowheads. "Indians had come from both north and south to hunt in Kentucky for many years before white settlers came. It was rich in game with much good water and salt licks." The arrowheads were bulky and full of grooves, a mix of light and dark sand-colored stones, with a few black points mixed in. Their tips were blunted now, but David could imagine a Cherokee hunter armed with a sheath of sharpened arrows, his body lithe and silent as he moved upwind of the game. David then thought of the broad-winged hawk that he saw on the fencepost as they exited the airport. It was as if that bird was keeping an eye on things; absurd maybe, but it felt as if the bird was a sort of gatekeeper waiting for the hunters to return.

The afternoon light came in sideways through the window, striking David in the eye. He moved into a smaller room off the main hall and nearly crashed into an assembly of plumb bobs. *What in the—?* They were painted white and organized according to size. *Ah yes, plumb bobs.* He had learned all about them in the Warehouse and Storage Logistics course during his second year at IFDM. It was the numbers and sheer mass that got David going. See, a typical warehouse stored around twenty thousand barrels. At five hundred-fifty pounds apiece, a full house would have about eleven million pounds of whiskey and barrel in it. On top of that, the warehouse itself would weigh about two million pounds—all in all, a tremendous weight on the foundation. The plum bob was, therefore, an essential tool to ensure the safety of the warehouse crew and the precious bourbon that had been so carefully made and stored.

David adored the simple physics: plumb bobs were hung from structural cross beams at four sites in a barrelhouse and aligned to vertical with a bubble level. Center plates were then fixed to the concrete foundation. If the warehouse structure shifted or leaned, anyone could see from the position of the bob to the plate which way the building was shifting and how far. Of course, warehouses were filled by a set pattern to ensure an even distribution of the weight of the full whiskey barrels—but one could never be sure how the structure and earth would respond.

David was beginning to enjoy himself here in this strange knick-knacky museum. Chuckling to himself, he moved on. Now here was a bizarre set up—a big old replica of a boot with a flask-like bottle tucked inside. "This bottle gave the word 'bootlegger' to the English language," the sign read. "It was carried in the leg of the boot by stage coach travelers and refilled at taverns along the route." *OK, sure, that's interesting*, thought David, *but why not use a real boot for the display?* Was the museum that short of funds? Or was the daughter of the curator some woebegone artist who they tried to appease by commissioning displays? David leaned in closer to see how the boot was made. *Was it paper-mache? Cardboard?* The crude paint made it hard to say...

The air in the room suddenly changed from the stuffy scent of dust to a faint smell of lilac and soap.

"Can I help you?"

David turned to face a blonde woman with a doughy complexion and dark, neglected roots. She was neither young nor old enough to reclaim any lost beauty that might have once whistled through her—and David doubted there had been any beauty to lose. He hummed a little melody of something he had heard somewhere in the day's travel. "Well, actually yes, maybe you can." He smiled and turned on the charm. "I'm David Dubehash from the Institute of Fermentation, Distillation, and Maturation in New York." He offered his hand.

"Pleased to meet you, Mr. Dubehash." She slipped a clammy palm into his. "My name is Flaget Nally. As curator here at the Oscar Getz Museum, I'd be happy to answer any questions you might have or guide you to anything of interest."

David looked down at her stockinged knees, then moved his eyes slowly back up to her eager brown eyes. "Well, Ms. Nally, I'm doing some research on eighteenth century strains of corn. Would you happen to have any information on varietals that would have been used for whiskey making around the mid 1700s?"

The curator's hand went to her mouth, where she proceeded to nibble on a short fingernail. "Well, um, I don't know. That's quite a long time ago, see and, well, we have a lot of information on nineteenth and twentieth century strains, but eighteenth? I'm afraid you have me stumped."

David didn't reply. He was looking past Flaget at a framed photo of a docked steamship. Workers—mostly black men—unloaded barrels at Old Darling Distillery in Carrollton, Kentucky. The men wore bowler hats and black button-up shirts. Some wore dark jackets and all had not shaven in many days. David couldn't tell if it was the quality of the photograph, his imagination, or the plain truth—but the men looked sooty, un-bathed, their boots heavy with mud, and their eyes wild with whiskey as they rolled the heavy barrels up the shore.

"Sir?"

"Yes, yes, sorry." David snapped out of it. "What about any old photographs of warehouses, or unique distilling equipment from that time period. Anything like that?"

Flaget lit up, eager to please. She took a step closer and spoke low. "Well, you could look through our archives. I'm not supposed to let anyone down there, but I'm workin' alone today, and if you don't tell anyone, I don't see why you couldn't take a wee peek."

"Why, Ms. Nally, you're a saint!" David clasped both her hands in his and bowed his forehead dramatically.

Flaget giggled and shook him off.

The Oscar Getz photo archives were, in fact, three file cabinets in the back corner of a mildewed basement crammed with foreboding lumps of canvas—presumably a valuable store of whiskey artifacts among a larger collection of junk. The photo files were organized by date, and after some tugging on the rusty drawers and cramming into a pair of too-small cotton gloves at the insistence of Ms. Nally, David located a file labeled 1850-1900—as far back as the photographs went.

He pulled it out, and with Ms. Nally tight on his heels, brought it upstairs to her undersized office and spread its contents onto the desk. One by one, David looked through the prints, unsure of what he was looking for. The file was thin. It held only five images—one daguerreotype on copper and four small prints on tin. The first was a portrait of a demonic-looking baby propped in a chair and wearing a long white baptism gown that pooled on the floor. David shuddered and thought about the ghosts at the inn. The second and third photographs were of the raising of a barn, a town's worth of men standing proud and straight-faced, while a blur of ropes and timber crowded the frame behind. The fourth was of a farmhouse and a family of men in overalls standing before it, along with several women. Or was that a woman and a child? He could not tell. The fifth was of St. Joseph's church before the statue was erected out front, when it was still flanked by wild fields and dust.

David stared, tapping his thumbs on the desk. Barclay's bourbon would have already been made and lost by the time these photos were taken, by the time photos *could* be taken for that matter, so what was he looking for? *There's nothing here.* David looked out the window onto the manicured lawn, then back at the photographs. *Nothing.* And yet, something was right there nagging at him. His eyes trolled over the photographs again, and stopped. *There.* The slightly hazy grass beside the farmhouse was not grass at all. It was corn.

David had grown up on a cereal farm in Ohio, and there had been cornfields nearby along the road to town. He knew what corn looked like, even on small traditional farms, and this wasn't it. The corn he knew had big ears and thin, long, strip-like leaves. The stalks were cane thick, like old cane poles for fishing in the creeks, in the canals, in the Miami-Eerie Canal where they hooked big mud-eating things—catfish or carp—which they fried over outdoor hickory fires, tossing the fish eyes in the pan first, just to see them skip and skittle in the heat. David hadn't thought of that in years.

The corn in this picture, however, was the exact opposite. It was hard to make out, but from what he could deduce, it had tiny ears with huge thick leaves. The stalks were tall, and the leaves flopped down to the roots, even with the mature ears.

The family posing for the photograph seemed odd as well. They looked, well, vibrant. Nobody smiled, not outright, but a few of the boys seemed to have a near grin approaching, something like a special knowledge and pride. And the women were beautiful, with thick hair and wild eyes that seemed to gaze out into the room despite the faded tones of the print.

David looked at the curator. If this wasn't a lead, there wasn't one in the place. Who was this family of ragtag farmers, with their down-home vixen? The matron in the photograph wore a high lace collar, her blouse was closed with pearl buttons—she did not sit, she stood with a strong, almost masculine stance—and she looked as untamed as a hawk.

The men wore overalls, though a few had changed into trousers with high waists and dark button-up shirts. A young girl in dark braids stood beside the woman, a slight scowl slick with mirth on her lips, and the sun, perhaps, in her eyes. The sun was in all of their eyes, it appeared, as David studied further, but it must have been an indirect autumnal light. No cameraman in those days would take a portrait with the sun in the subjects' eyes. The time required to keep the aperture open was too long.

Also it must have been fall when the photograph was taken, because the corn behind them was mature. The men were cleaned up, but their implements were dirty, so David figured the photo was taken in the late afternoon, after working from sunup, having had the afternoon meal, when the maturing sun would have taken on that sleepy reflective quality, such as there was now outside the museum. This sensation of fading light mixed with an apprehension in David to figure out who this family was and what they still knew about corn, if their descendants were still in Kentucky, or in existence at all.

David looked at Flaget, that lonely heart, and smiled. He liked her, somewhat more, certainly a touch more now than he had at first, albeit she was going to stay Flaget Nally of the Oscar Getz Museum of Whiskey History, and nothing further, in his book.

"Ms. Nally?" he asked. "You know who these folks are?" The men were as handsome as the women comely, and they held hand-fashioned rakes and hoes in their considerable fists. They had decided to be photographed with the implements of their work. Perhaps it was no decision at all, but instinct, much as David's grandfather had always preferred to be photographed at work. David smiled at the memories. Seed hats, short-sleeved work shirts, a tractor. An IH, or a John Deere in the years before David left. Beechnut in the front shirt pocket. Go back far enough, and you'd see one of David's ancestors with a two-man horse-drawn corn dropper, or before that, a mule and plow drawn in charcoal or left unrendered.

"The Stillwaters?" Flaget asked, as if David should already know their name. David gave Flaget an encouraging eye. He was enjoying this little game of teasing her with his attention.

"Flaget, you think you could help me with something?" David coydogged.

"Ask me."

"Is Nally a local name?"

"Local as all the names around here."

"Do any of the Stillwaters still live around here?"

"Why's that, Mr. David, eh…Sorry. Remind me of your last name."

"I think they might know something about what I'm looking for," he said. "And it's Dubehash." Flaget came closer and let her shoulder brush against David's bicep. He could smell her budget perfume.

"Perley Stillwater, the great-great-great-granddaughter of that woman in the photograph, why she lives just a few blocks away. I could walk you there when I get off."

"Oh, no, no, that won't be necessary. I can manage. Where's her house exactly? Just point the way."

CHAPTER TWELVE

Walking into ZAK Cooperage, Sam was met with a blast of hot air, fragrant with burning white oak. It was one of Samuel's favorite smells: the charring of barrels, a simple aroma akin to fresh bread. The warm greeting was followed by a hearty welcome from a man in a double-ply work shirt, his sleeves rolled to expose thick forearms.

"Dugranval!" Rick Perry yelled as Sam made his way up the drive. "Is that Parker's car? You lucky dog." Rick was a grizzly of a man, his bulk at odds with his kindly eyes and agile gate. Rick slung an arm over Sam's shoulders and ushered him into the building through an open barn-sized door.

"I've come to check on my wood," Sam said, his shoes sounding on the concrete as they stepped inside. Though he was happy to see Rick, he felt entirely unable to muster up a jovial mood.

"Well it's 'bout time," Rick said. "It's only been sittin' here for eighteen months." Then he noticed Samuel's expression. "Hey I heard the news about Campbell. It's unbelievable. Really, I'm sorry, Sam. I know you two were close."

"I appreciate that, I do," said Sam, his big brown eyes looking up at Rick earnestly, vulnerably. "Though maybe we weren't as close as I thought. The whole thing, well, I don't know what to think or feel."

Rick nodded, letting Sam leave it at that, and the two men walked past a short conveyor belt where a teenager with earbuds tucked under his noise-cancellation headphones watched freshly cut staves go by, checking the wood for flaws.

"Goggles!" Rick yelled at him, but the kid couldn't hear. "I swear, one of these days that punk is goin' to get a sliver in the eye."

They turned left and walked the main floor of the cooperage where several men methodically hammered rings onto staves with rubber pallets, softly, yet firmly, coaxing the barrels into shape. Behind them, men with torches set fire to the insides of the bowed cylinders, Samuel counting out the seconds they let the wood burn, determining the charcoal layer of these barrels at grade 3. For a surprising eighty seconds (nearly double the standard time), the thin flames greedily licked the virgin wood. Over the years, as the whiskey matured, those eighty seconds would make a world of difference. Originally used as a means of disinfecting barrels that were reused, this charring process had a serendipitous effect on the corn whiskey as it aged during the long river transports from Kentucky to New Orleans. Whiskey readily seeps into the wood through the porous char, which filters out much of the sulfuric flavors and allows the liquid to come into contact with a caramelized 'red layer' of wood beneath, enhancing the sweet notes, and of course, imparting the signature bourbon hue.

"Well are you coming or not?" asked Rick, giving Samuel a knowing look, a tentative tease.

Rick and Samuel had known each other for nearly fourteen years. Back when Sam was fresh out of graduate school, he did an apprenticeship with Dewey Bordes, husband of Mrs. B., and had spent six months in Kentucky learning the ins and outs of what it took to be a master distiller of bourbon. Dewey Bordes was a man who only sourced the best materials for his craft, and he had always ordered barrels from Rick's father, Earnest Perry, the founder of ZAK. Samuel had remained a faithful customer ever since. Furthermore Rick shared Samuel's love of wood on a deeper level that not many in the world did.

Sam gave a weak smile, as if to excuse himself for dawdling. His mind lingered a moment longer on the unique charm of charred wood, his body detached from the world, numbed with the presence of death. Had no one been around, Sam might just have climbed into one of those freshly toasted barrels. It would be the ideal environment to curl up in and disappear—entombed in that warm and lulling smell.

Sam followed Rick out another large door to the back of the building where a small timber yard rested in the shade of early dusk. Samuel was prepping an experiment here. Though wood for bourbon barrels is typically laid out in temperature-controlled predryers for a month, he was having a selection of wood air-seasoned—the French way. The fresh air would enhance the wood by allowing the development of a variety of mildews that reduced astringency and converted the wood's lignin into vanillin. In wine, this reduced some of the harsher tannins, and in whiskey, it led to a sweeter, mellower taste (particularly because American white oak has a lower tannic content than the European woods used for wine).

But Samuel was not going to use this wood for barrels. He was preparing the staves for a fan assembly—a construction that he would submerge into whiskey within a stainless steel tank at IFDM. The experiment was to test a series of different wood configurations and surface area ratios, along with the use of "micro-oxygenation" and precise pressure control, to see how to best replicate the taste of a true barrel-aged spirit.

"I wonder about the humidity here," said Sam, taking a walk around his stacked wood. "I hear it's been a dry fall." *The wood smells a bit too clean, too much like wood, a little peppery, not earthy enough.*

"Well it sure ain't France, I can tell you that," Rick chided. "But I think your precious molds are doing just fine."

"I'll have to take a sample to be sure." Sam leaned toward the pile and breathed in. *Yes, the wood needs more time, another winter to expand what little moisture was there, and a spring for it to thaw and break up.*

"I'll get one of my men to take care of it," said Rick. "Hey, you doin' all right? I have a bottle in my office. It's been a while since you and I caught up. What do you say we have ourselves a drink?"

From the top drawer of his cherry desk, Rick pulled out a bottle of Single Barrel Eagle Rare. Aged for over ten years to an exquisite crimson hue, every bottle was different than the next, each bearing the unique profile of the barrel from which it came, each a subtle variation on the consistent Eagle Rare theme. This was exactly what Sam needed: something bold, dry, and full of oak. The wood-slat shades in the office windows striated the sunlight across the floor as Rick poured a few fingers into two small rocks glasses, handed one to Sam, and leaned against his desk. Rick was the kind of man who rarely sat, a creature more at ease on his feet.

Samuel, meanwhile, had all but collapsed into a chair. It was as if the comfort of a good friend, in an environment that made him feel at home and secure, suddenly made him release all of the composure that had kept him functioning throughout the day. He unbuttoned his suit jacket and sighed. More than anything, Sam felt exhausted. He let the sweet leathery aroma of the bourbon calm him and tried to clear his mind of thoughts.

"Do you know what a symbolic birth cabin is?" Rick asked, giving Sam a wry, eyebrowed look.

"A what?"

"They built a cabin there over at Abraham Lincoln National Historical Park—they're callin' it a symbolic birth cabin. It's supposed to represent the cabin Abe was born in, but it sounds like a load of bull to me."

"Tourism," said Sam, perking up a little. "There are some things I don't understand. It seems people nowadays like their history *toute faite*, ready-made. People don't know how to use their imagination anymore, not when traveling. They just want to take a photograph and then go eat lunch."

"If they really wanted to know 'bout Lincoln's childhood, they would be bringin' me *my* lunch here!" said Rick. "Either that, or maybe we should just throw 'em into Knob Creek out back and let them flap 'round for a while in the water before draggin' them in."

The ZAK Cooperage and Stavemill was located just off of Knob Creek on a parcel of land that had once been a several-hundred acre farm—a modest thirty acres of which was home to the Lincoln clan. Abraham lived on that land from when he was two until he was eight years old, and back then, the building in which Sam and Rick were now drinking was a distillery owned by Wattie Boone. Abe's father, Thomas Lincoln, had worked in that distillery, and Rick was always mentioning how young Abe was said to have hiked the mile or so to the distillery every day to bring his father lunch. Eventually young Abe was also put to work sweeping the distillery floors, cleaning the tanks, and performing other simple tasks.

Samuel smiled. "I had forgotten that story about Lincoln falling into Knob Creek. He was playing on a footbridge, right? And his schoolmate pulled him out with a branch." Samuel took a sip of his drink (he had been nosing it for some time). The lingering dryness he had expected was there, and as he swallowed, a hint of rich cocoa and candied almonds swelled up from underneath. Some people felt that you shouldn't age a bourbon for more than ten years because the oak would overpower the whiskey if it stayed in the barrel too long, but Sam could imagine this particular batch becoming quite delightful with the spice and oak it would get from maturing for another year or two.

"You know, everyone thinks Lincoln was a temperance man," Sam mused, "but I disagree. I think he was simply a man of moderation. During the Civil War, after the battle of Shiloh, or I should say after the failure of the battle of Shiloh, everyone was calling General Grant an alcoholic. But Lincoln defended him, and he did so in a way that I think is absolutely brilliant, not to mention kind of whimsical for such a serious president. Lincoln interrupted a Missouri congressman, Henry T. Blow, I think, as Blow was going on and on about the drinking habits of Grant. Lincoln cut him off and said, 'I wish I knew what brand of whiskey he drinks. I would send a barrel to all my other generals.'"

Rick laughed. "A smart man. Very smart. Back when this here place was a distillery and that little Abe was runnin' around helpin' out, you know old Wattie Boone took a liking to him. He could tell Abe would become a great man and, of course, Wattie being a Kentucky Boone and all, he was hopin' Abe would go into distilling. He even went so far as to say that if Abe went into the whiskey biz, he'd be the best distiller in the U.S."

Sam had heard this story before, but he didn't mind hearing it again. The possibility of Lincoln growing up to become a distiller pleased him as well. It made him feel almost righteous even, as if understanding the art of distilling was a sign of nobility. He imagined young Lincoln on his back in the grass not far from here, listening to his mother read from the Bible and letting his mind drift up into the oak branches framing the sky. Surely Lincoln as a boy must have felt some innate understanding of the potential that oak held, of what his father did all day, of what a proper grasp of materials, diligence, patience, and finesse could yield. Surely there was some inkling of this in his forming mind, a budding awareness of how to extract the best from both nature and man.

Sam was feeling nostalgic, sad. Rick Perry was right there with him, his compassionate eyes reading everything as he poured them each another drink.

Woodrow Campbell, too, had an aptitude for drawing out the goodness in materials, whatever their source. Give him a taste of white dog, and Campbell would tell you how to make that spirit reach its fullest potential in five, ten, thirty years. Campbell understood wood too; his appreciation for oak had been deep and tactile. In fact, Woodrow Campbell and Rick Perry were the only two people (not including family, meaning Lydia, David, and Mrs. B.) to whom Samuel had divulged the whereabouts of his tree house in the Ozarks—his rustic penthouse refuge, an escape that was luxurious in materials, construction, and comfort, yet sparse in modern amenities, technology, and noise. Sam wished he was there now.

"Hey, you never told me why you came to Kentucky in the first place," Rick said, a deliberate pull on Sam to keep him from dwelling too much on his thoughts. "I know you didn't come all the way here just to see me. Or your wood for that matter. I could have easily shipped that sample." Rick let the corner of his mouth curl up playfully on one side.

"You're right, I never did tell you. You're going to love this. I can't believe it was only yesterday. It feels like so much time has passed. Well, it was beautiful, Richard, you should have been there. I tasted the most exquisite whiskey. It was unearthed from beneath the World Trade Center site, from this old ship an excavator dug out. We think the bottle was from the time of the revolution or earlier. Pure corn too. But it was aged, which, as you know, was unheard of back then—and yet there was something else to it, a certain *je ne sais quoi*, something more than just time and corn. You could see it too. The color was such a dark red, but bright at the same time. A thick color, but the liquid wasn't thick. Do you know of any chemical reaction that would produce something like that?"

"What a find! Are you sure it was aged in oak?" Rick asked. "I mean, it could have been aged in somethin' else—pine or rubber—somethin' not quite as pure as oak, somethin' with resin canals."

"No, no, it tasted like oak, and the chemical analysis points to oak. It was more like somehow all of that time had brightened the flavors and color somehow. Made them come more alive."

"Maybe it was aged in chestnut oak or post oak instead of white oak." Rick had become serious, his eyes narrowing as he searched for ideas. "Both chestnut and post have higher levels of hemicellulose. More hemicellulose would make for a darker color, especially if the barrel was charred, but I don't know. I would think the color after all that time would be more brown, not bright red."

"Exactly. The numbers didn't suggest more hemicellulose, and really, the difference between white oak and chestnut or post isn't enough to create that much of a difference, even after all of that time." Samuel was frustrated. He had hoped Rick would be able to shed light on something he had overlooked or something he did not fully understand. But Rick's mind was only running all of the same possibilities Sam's had—and there wasn't enough of Barclay's bourbon for Rick to get a firsthand look or taste.

Sam was feeling testy, exhausted. He felt like driving out to this cooperage had been a waste. He didn't know anything more about Barclay's bourbon than when he had first arrived in Kentucky, and the idea of aged whiskey dating so far back seemed impossible, so against all that he knew of the potent stuff they made back then, so far from the considerations of that time when whiskey was meant to be consumed quickly. *But why not? Why wouldn't some people who may have liked the French-aged brandy, already imported in the mid-eighteenth century to the United States, decide to apply the same technique of maturation to whiskey?*

Sam could "what if" forever, but nothing could change the fact that Woodrow Campbell was dead. Sam felt overwhelmed, frustrated. He needed to sleep.

"There's something else I wanted to talk to you about, Rick," he said. "The paper said that the tensions between the local distilleries and the Japanese conglomerates were running high. What did Woody get himself mixed up in?"

CHAPTER THIRTEEN

This was not the house. Not the land from the photograph either. There was no corn, no old brick homestead, and David lost hope. Had he really expected to find corn growing outside the home of whomever Stillwater he found? In town, besides? Yes, he supposed he had. And would Perley be a young Stillwater? Would she look like the woman in the photograph? *Stillwater*, David thought, seeing the name on the mailbox. Stillwater. That was an old bourbon name! Some old lost brand, he was sure of it.

He hoped Perley was a looker. If she was not, or if she were married, then there were only two things to look forward to that night: one was staying in his room alone with an old ghost for a roommate; the other, calling Flaget.

It was good being here for Sam, but David hadn't even tasted Barclay's old bourbon. Now Woody was murdered, Samuel was depressed, and Kentucky felt ominous. In town, he had seen some big men, none of whom looked friendly, and some who glared with outright hatred. David knew the men of this part of the world. If they weren't drinking, and even more so if they *were* drinking, they were looking for a fight. Women came third, often not at all, for these big flat-headed boys. A truck went by with no muffler, making a hell of a noise. David was on the porch of a house and had no idea what he would say to Perley, looker or not.

The house was a two-story historic colonial, sided in yellow aluminum. It had a cement front porch, painted red with four metal latticework pillars. David scuffed his shoe on the front mat and twisted the turnkey of the bell upon the door. It circled its dinging sounds, but didn't sound promising. He heard a car backfire, or maybe it was a gunshot. He ducked slightly, rung the bell again, and cleared his throat. A scattering of birds flew past. Sparrows. There were no lights on inside. No car in the driveway.

A light appeared at the window nearest the door. The door opened slightly, and was suddenly opened all the way, revealing a gorgeous creature of the rarest breed, standing quite tall. She was a Stillwater through and through. Her hair was gray and thick, pulled in a tight bun, a few strands falling down her face and along her collarbone. She had faint earlobes and a long graceful neck. Olive complexioned, her eyes shone dark green with yellow rings around her deep pupils, and the irises were complex and rich. She had high cheekbones, a few freckles, and was probably seventy years old, at least.

Damn, thought David. If only they had been born in the same era, surely they would have been lovers. She put one foot behind the other, clearly not afraid of a strange man in the near dark. He smelled plumeria. He caught a scent of clean and tilled earth as if from the cereal farm on which he had grown up. She was stunning. A thoroughbred. A standardbred, though there was nothing standard about the woman. No, there had been nothing lost through breeding; in fact, she was in all ways the glowing light of the woman he'd been captivated by in the photograph, and then some.

"Who are you?" David heard himself say, though he knew it was she who should be asking that question of him. His handsome cheeks reddened as he forced a boyish smile. "Perley? Perley Stillwater?" David asked.

She was well so well featured and healthy—her distinctly colored eyes offset by a white blouse, a blue skirt—that he couldn't tell her age. She shifted her heel to stand hips-width apart, strong and lean. He smiled, dumbly, and stuck his hand out. "I'm David."

"Well hello, David. What do you want?" she asked as if she were ready to dismiss him. Maybe she thought he was a door-to-door salesman? A census official? A steam cleaner of carpets? David stammered a bit. Cleared his throat. God, she was extraordinary. And such legs she still had. Was she a looker or had she been a looker, which was it?

"I'm interested in corn," David began. He looked down, looked up, and was doing his silly game. She feigned as if to close the door.

"What do you want?" she said again, and almost shut him out. "Why are you here?"

"I found a photo of you, of your ancestors. Stillwaters." David straightened up. "At the Getz museum today. I am a chemist. I work in Manhattan at a university of distillation. I'm doing some research on unique strains of corn, and I was hoping to talk to you about old, perhaps no longer even in existence, types of local corn."

She eased up. "Well, come on in, young man. Relax. I'll put some water on, and we can talk about corn till the sun comes up. I know more than my share. Can I get you a drink?"

"Thank you. Anything is fine," David said. He would be wise to play this cool. "Will you have one with me?"

Inside the cheaply finished exterior of the home, Perley had worked miracles. There were no crosses or photographs of grandchildren, no gewgaws or needlepointed quotes or gaudy mirrors, none of the other trappings of poor taste with which the old are often saddled. Instead David found a naturally dyed and warmly faded Afghan rug. Her round kitchen table was a large slab of oak, which had been taken as a slice of an entire trunk, and upon the table shone sterling candlesticks with handmade beeswax candles.

Perley got a bottle. It bore no label, no emblem on the glass. She placed, with a firm hand, a shallow water glass before David and another at her place. A small lamp in a corner of the countertop lit the room, and a standing lamp near her side of the table illuminated an antique smoker, upon which rested a silver ashtray with a few discarded cigarettes. Perley was a smoker. David liked this.

She poured the drinks. No ice. Straight unaged whiskey, white dog. It was moonshine. David grinned. "Thank you, Ms. Stillwater."

"Don't come around a home in Bardstown and expect anything less," she winked. "Nor tolerate. Now what's your full name, David, and what are you hopin' to find out about corn? I assume you know the basics? Furthermore I don't like a man showin' up unannounced at my home after sundown. You're lucky I am an old woman. In my younger days, I would have chased you off my property with a shotgun." David smiled and so did she, then her voice got quieter. "Of course, this isn't really my property. This is just the house I live in now," her eyes danced and she took a swallow. "Anyhow," she said, "speak."

"The last name is Dubehash. I know the basics of corn. I was raised by farmers a state over. I wasn't always a city boy," he winked, took a polite sip, and managed to keep a neutral face when the strength of the moonshine hit his tongue. He settled back into the covered cushion of the chair, the alcohol heating his nose and throat, the warmth spreading though his body. He liked white dog. He rather liked looking at Perley, too, seeing the younger woman she once was coming through. "I saw the photograph of the old Stillwater farm at the Getz Museum, where a young lady told me about you and where to find you. I apologize for showing up at sundown. I only arrived in Kentucky late this afternoon. And it is nice to sit and have a drink. Ms. Stillwater, thank you."

"Go on."

"So here it is. A few days ago, a very old bottle of bourbon was introduced to myself and my mentor at IFDM—that's the school where I work—and we believe that the bourbon was made with a very old strain of corn. I noticed the corn in the photograph of the old Stillwater farm, and I know old corn some. But I thought maybe you would know...I don't know what I was thinking. I needed to talk to someone who is from here, who would know the old corn varieties that the natives would have introduced, and that the first Kentucky farmers would have grown and possibly distilled."

"Finish up that drink, young man, and get out of here. You don't know anything about corn. You shouldn't have come here."

David taken aback. He sat up. "Then teach me about corn," he said. "I want to know as much as you can tell me."

"GMO. That's all that anyone cares about anyhow. Why don't you just go and talk to the Monsanto farmers, those sons of bitches with their self-destructing seeds. Go talk to the corn farmers all around here, all of them using that smut. The few good farmers we had have been overrun by the corporations—a bunch of cheap suits found the

Monsanto genes mixed in with the local corn and took farmer to court for intellectual property. Intellectual property—corn! That is the furthest thing from intelligence or intellect I have ever heard of. Finish your drink. Then go home to New York City. What do you know? You're a boy. Kentucky doesn't need you, and you don't need Kentucky."

She was even more beautiful worked up like this. "Perley, you're right. Sure you are. I don't know enough. I do need to know about corn. Not GMO corn either. I wish it were stricken from the face of the earth. I read in a journal about turquoise corn—stuff with small ears and deep green kernels. You ever heard of anything like that?"

"No. Corn around here was never like that. It was all either brought by the native tribes hundreds of years ago, long before white people came, or it came from new England. I'll tell you this, the natives who came here—the Cherokee, the Shawnee, the Yuchi, and the Chickasaw—they all had their strains of corn. It all started in Mexico. Mexico before it was Mexico, when the natives there learned the ways of teosinte."

"Yes, I know about teosinte. I know that maize came from grass and was bred into corn over a thousand years of domestication and migration south of the border six thousand years ago. That teosinte has many branches instead of a central stalk and that teosinte has several male flowers, whereas corn has only one per stalk at the top."

"You don't know anything. South of the border. What border? How did grass turn into corn? You're the chemist. How did this happen? I have read many expert reports and studies arguin' passionately everything from hand selection, to introgression, to hybridization, but no one really understands how this miracle occurred! The first maize had eight rows of kernels and was a few inches long. I'll tell you this too, David! Every strain of corn we have, we have because of a story. It is stories that turn one strain into another. The stories of generations after generations in a family and all the intermixing with other families, other races, that have spread and kept each strain of corn alive. Ever heard of Bloody Butcher corn? Go over to West Virginia, meet with Edgar Meadows, and he'll tell you the whole story. Eight generations in his family back to the Cherokees who stole his great-great-great-great-great-great-grandmother. But within a few dozen years, you will destroy all of this—you 'chemists' with your Bt Corn and Roundup Ready, and who will ever know anything? And you want to come in and find out all about corn, the history of corn in Kentucky, and all of the Native American tribes that brought their kernels in pouches sewn together out of husks, or in skins, and then you'll leave in what? An hour? Two hours? Catch a plane? For what reason? What do you know about wildflowers, David?"

"Um, nothing really. Some. Not much."

"What do you know much about, young man?"

"Chemistry. Whiskey. How to ferment, and distill, and mature alcohol. I know that some. Pretty well, in fact."

"Well here's to that," she said and finished her drink in a throaty gulp. She seemed to think for a moment and look him over. "David, you are going to have to talk to my granddaughter," David's ears perked up, and his face beamed. "I know what you're thinking, and don't even think about it, David!" Perley laughed. "She's as fierce as the winter day is short. And she has the Stillwater temper." Perley stood and put her hand on the back of her chair. Then she moved decidedly to the phone mounted on the wall. "Is it just you, alone, in town?" Perley asked before she picked up the receiver.

"No, my mentor is here with me. His name is Samuel Dugranval."

"Dungrun-what? Well fine. Shh! Clara." Perley stuck out her tongue at David. "I have a young man here. He's good lookin', and I insist you two meet. He's a chemist from New York City." She tapped her foot, and David could hear the voice from the other end, clearly not happy. "I don't care about any of that. He wants to know about corn, and he seems genuinely interested in old corn strains for making good whiskey. You're going to have him over for coffee tomorrow morning. No. He's here with me now. Clara. That's enough of that, Clara. You'll see him tomorrow morning. I'll give him directions."

Perley poured them each another drink. "I want to tell you one more thing, young man. Just as you cannot separate corn, and each strain of corn, from the lineage of the people who worked with it, lived with it, grew it, so you cannot separate the stories from the tribes who lived in Kentucky. I mean, not that you cannot separate the natives from the state, because you nearly can, and that pretty well happened, but you literally cannot pull the stories apart. They all blur together. For instance, take the Cherokee, who have many stories about corn." She topped off their glasses. "My family has remembered these stories as my family was here all the way back then, nearly. The Cherokee say there was a corn woman. One day, the corn woman went to the storeroom, and she told some boys to stand away and not follow, but they followed. They watched her from the cracks in the wall while she was inside. They saw her rub her body, and corn filled her basket. Selu—that was this corn woman—she knew they had seen her. She said because they had seen her, they would die at the end of their lives, and with them so would the easy life of being fed by the Selu. She told them to drag her body seven times around a circle in front of their house and over the soil. Then the story goes on to tell how the animals were upset with man for hunting them. So the animals decided that if a hunter did not pray, he would get diseases from the animals' meat. This happened so much, the men gettin' diseases, that the plants took pity on the humans moaning in the forest. The corn took the most pity, but not only corn. Many plants learned to help humans to combat all the plagues that the animals gave them. But look, you're a chemist. We know better, right." She winked. They finished their glasses, and she lifted the bottle again.

CHAPTER FOURTEEN

Samuel waited for David at the restaurant within the Old Talbott Inn. He sat at a squat table of lacquered oak in a sack-back, unpadded oak chair. The room had low ceilings, wood paneling, and held a dozen tables, none of which held other guests. If only he were in New York—there he and David could share a decent meal, have a few glasses of good wine, and then he could crawl into bed with Lydia.

David was late. What a horrible day it had been. He hoped David's lateness meant he had discovered something about corn, not that David had once again found himself a woman. Samuel sipped wine from a fingerprint-smeared glass—the selection was the poorest he had seen in years. For Merlot, they had Kendall Jackson, for Cabernet they had Papio. And the Shiraz selection was Yellowtail. He knew better, and yet he'd ordered the Papio.

Some men got drunk when all was wrong. Some busted their knuckles against a wall or got themselves into trouble, but Samuel was merely drinking this bad wine. It was self-punishment, Papio.

A wedged particle of cork floated on the surface of his glass. He should have had a beer. Sam reviewed the menu and thought about Lydia, her pale French neck and clean features. He thought of her scent, remembered it bodily. Aspects of her person he could not articulate but could feel within himself, as one might recall certain feelings of childhood, like coming in from the chill of autumn orchards into the warmth of the family coat room.

This was, and was not, the feeling he had with Lydia. Lydia was… Samuel knew he could not attempt to put into words the feelings of being with her, how he disappeared when he was with her, and reappeared, and how she did too. And they became one sharing a table, or in their fine bed, or brushing their teeth together in the bathroom. It was impossible to place, yet it was everywhere. It was something about how they traveled together, how they were at home together, a certain way in which even without her, she was with him. He saw through her eyes as well as his own, the world they shared full of stories and memories they both held illuminated, as like anything behind a glass lit from within. Samuel was staring at the ensconced flame of the oil lamp within beveled glass on the oak table.

He inhaled through his nose and pushed the acidic glass of wine away, deciding to switch to something else as soon as David arrived. *Where is he?*

The phone rang, and Sam answered. It was Lydia, and he was slightly awed.

"Hello, my hen," he said, "I was just thinking of you. It's been a rough day."

"Samuel, don't you ever think to call your wife?" Lydia cooed. "What's wrong? How is the land of bourbon?"

"Well, Lydia...I don't know how else to say this. Woodrow Campbell died this morning. He was...he was murdered. I'm sorry. God, I'm sorry. But he's been killed."

"Jesus, Samuel, are you OK?" Her voice was complex and sturdy. "What happened?" She was there for him. It wasn't the sort of "being there" other people pretended with their "I'm so sorrys," which only showed their own weaknesses, but it was really her being there with him, coming together, as if in prayer, even though Sam was not a praying man.

"It's going to be all right, Lydia. I'm fine. Today was awful, but I'm safe. Someone attacked Woodrow with a knife at a distillery early this morning. We don't know anything else yet, but we are going to figure out who did this."

Lydia whispered something Sam could not make out.

"David is here to give me a hand," he said. "Don't worry, Lydia. I love you."

"Should I—Do you want me to come down there?"

"No, really, it's fine. Everything will be fine. Just take care of Leo. Tell him I'll bring him back something from Kentucky."

David walked unsteadily into the entrance of the inn.

"David just walked into the lobby. He looks drunk. Can I call you in a few hours from my room? I have secret things I want to tell you regarding what I want to do with you when I get home from this trip."

David wove his way through the lobby, talking sideways to the girl in the velour jumpsuit at the desk, then hit his head on the low door-frame, ducked, swore, held his forehead, and fell into the sack-backed chair across from Sam's.

"What is this, some kind of funhouse?" David said, laughing and holding his forehead. "Everything here is too low to the floor. It's an inn for little people. How tall was Jesse James? How tall was Lincoln, for Chrissakes, under that hat? I've got a strong buzz going, Samuel, let's keep it that way! How are you? You look like hell, no offense." David slapped a hand on the table. "I met a woman," he announced.

The waitress came round, and Samuel ordered the Old Kentucky Hot Brown, which was described as smoked turkey and sugar-cured baked Virginia ham on toast, smothered in Mornay sauce and melted cheddar cheese, topped with bacon and tomato. He could not believe he had ordered it, as so many flavors in one dish would surely wreak havoc on his tastebuds. David ordered prime rib with "Stagecoach Fries." Samuel realized he needed to catch up with David and ordered a Sazerac with Mitchter's Rye, passing his wine across the table. The waitress left and David fidgeted with his legs.

"David, sit still," Samuel ordered. "Before I have to hear about another woman you've met, I want to tell you what Rick Perry told me at ZAK Cooperage toda—"

"I met Perley Stillwater," David began.

"Wait. He said about two months ago when Woody returned from Japan, a bunch of Suntory guys..."

"Who's that?"

"Rick. Rick said a bunch of these Japanese guys were looking for a warehouse...Wait. You met who?"

"The most beautiful older woman I have ever laid eyes on. And she…" David took a large sip of Sam's wine, then stuck his tongue out to pluck a piece of cork off its tip.

The waitress delivered the Sazerac, and Sam sniffed over the mix, as if to escape from his partner. "They overdid the bitters," Sam said with a stern look, thinking in a loud voice. "It's no better here than in New York City where the 'mixologists' play too much with bitters, making cocktails as if prohibition were still in effect, as if it were necessary to mask vice with bitters and fruit." Sam sighed. "And what's the matter with this Perley Stillwater?" David had started eating his salad ravenously.

"She is the grandmother of our breakfast date tomorrow morning," David said, chewing up a ring of red onion. Samuel lifted his eyebrows, sipping on his aperitif.

"Hold on a sec," David said and ran to the bathroom.

By the time David returned, the Hot Brown had arrived, along with the prime rib. "Perley knows all about native corn, I am pretty sure," David mumbled somewhere behind his prime rib, chewing the words along with the meat. "Actually I saw a picture of Perley Stillwater's ancestors at the museum, and the curator—a charming lady named Flaget—told me where she lived." David seemed to recover some of his wits with the prime rib. "Perley is a spitfire of a woman, Sam. But I got her—don't ask me how—to set us up with a date to meet her grand-daughter tomorrow morning to learn all about native corn."

"And?" inquired Dugranval.

David felt suddenly alone and foolish in the old inn's dining room. That was all. He didn't answer.

Samuel sighed, and they finished the meal in silence. Samuel paid the check and headed toward the Lincoln Suite off the main foyer.

David muttered good night and found his way to the hallway leading to the door of the Anton Heinrich room. Before David had reached the door, he smelled cigar smoke and thought of the ghost-infested chair, and of the foolish woman in the jumpsuit. He entered the key into the lock and turned it, wishing he could have gotten the Jesse James room or any other room in the inn or at another inn in town. The smell of that cigar smoke was strong, and there was no smoke anywhere to cause it.

CHAPTER FIFTEEN

He stood at the door politely, his hat in his hand.

Samuel tightened the knot on his bathrobe, "I should have guessed."

"May I come in, Mr. Dugranval?" Agent Lefevre asked.

"Just ask your questions, and I'll do what I can to answer them," Sam opened the door wider and took a step back.

Lefevre walked in slowly, scanning the Lincoln Suite and running a hand along the plastered fireplace mantle. He pulled out the chair from the writing desk and took a seat, gesturing toward an armchair for Sam to do the same.

Sam shut the door and remained standing by it.

"I just came from Parker Beam's," Lefevre started, setting his hat onto an antique writing desk. Without the glasses, his eyes looked much older than his face. "He told me you flew into Kentucky yesterday. Tell me, what's your business here?"

"I'm doing research for a client in New York."

Lefevre nodded slowly. "Wouldn't happen to be research for that whiskey-swapping trial, now would it? One of Suntory's distilleries—Yamazaki, I believe—has a stake in that?"

"Well if you know about it, you know I'm not at liberty to talk about it." Sam walked over to the bed and took a sip from a water glass on the nightstand.

Lefevre stood up. "Parker Beam said you two got quite drunk last night. Said he couldn't be sure if you went straight to bed or went out."

"Look, friend." Sam put the glass down. "You may be the FBI, and I may have walked into a horrible situation down here in Kentucky, but don't bluff me. I've lost a very dear colleague today."

Lefevre didn't answer immediately. He traced his steps back to the mantle and studied a small bust of Lincoln that served as a bookend. "Well I guess you'd like to know," he said as he pulled out a book on the history of Bardstown, "that Four Roses distillery will commence production again tomorrow." He eyes rose from the book to Sam. "Though I wouldn't mind if it stayed shut down."

Sam pursed his lips in annoyance. "And why would that be? Are you allergic to corn?"

"In addition to my federal duties, Mr. Du—or should I call you The Flying Distiller? In addition to my federal post, I head up the local chapter of the New Temperance Society."

"You must read my monthly newsletter on fine spirits." Sam almost smiled, but thought better of it. "No one in Kentucky calls me The Flying Distiller."

Lefevre had the book open, but he wasn't reading it. "I've done my research on you. Seems that trouble always shows up where you are, and though I would not want to imply that most crimes are due to intemperance, certainly temperance has never failed to reduce their number."

Sam had had enough. "I said I'd cooperate. You know damn well I'm not involved in Woody's murder—"

"Do I?" Lefevre, interrupted, smiling lazily.

"Because I'm not. Surely Linda and Parker vouched for my where-abouts last night. And your forensics team must have noticed the foot-prints in Woodrow's blood, which you certainly gathered are not my size. And besides, Woodrow and I are on the same team, we hold the same ideals, which is more than I can say of our little relationship."

Lefevre twisted his smile in a little deeper and sat back down in the chair, lifting one leg over the other. "OK, Mr. Dugranval, you seem to know everything. I've run through all things you mentioned. Your alibi checks out. And it's true, this murder doesn't seem in keeping with your nature. We're not after you. It's just that we can't afford to pass up any angles."

"Good. Then what did you come here for?"

"What do you know about Rob Hutchins? He skipped town right after the murder, caught a flight to Vegas."

Sam nodded. "You really don't have anything do you? I know that he's been a loyal employee of Parker Beam at Heaven Hill for over six years now. I can't think of any possible reason he'd have it out for Woody."

"You're going to stick with that story?"

"What else?"

Lefevre rolled his tongue over his cheek in thought, then slowly stood up. "Well I just hope you aren't making any mistakes." He fetched his hat. "Good night for now. I'll be talking to you soon."

CHAPTER SIXTEEN

There was a blaring noise and billows of steam. He was trying to say something, but no sound would come out. David opened an eye. The phone was ringing. *Gah!* He picked up the receiver and slammed it down again. He looked over, and there was no one in bed but himself. He didn't feel like he understood. Where was…?

He had slept alone, of course, but throughout the night, in moments nearing wakefulness, the sense had come upon him, departed, and come again of someone sleeping in his bed beside him. Someone pulling on the covers, a movement of breathing, perhaps sensed in a hypnologic state. The phone began to ring again.

"All right, all right, I'm up."

Light was coming in through the horrible blinds. Early Kentucky light, flat and dull, hitting the old floral wallpaper. He got up and started looking for his pants. The phone rang again. It was Sam.

Oh, yes, he had a date this morning, David remembered. He went to the sink, pulled the metal handle up and splashed water on his face, failing to look straight at his eyes in the mirror. He did a quick splash under his arms as well and smiled for the girl he would meet—a Stillwater. He put on his shirt and shoes and left the room, checking to make sure the door was locked before heading downstairs to meet Sam.

A cup of coffee and a few sweet beignets were waiting on a table for him. Sam was also waiting, his coffee nearly finished, the newspaper beside him, folded closed, the word "Roses" semiobscured by a plate of half-eaten eggs and stone ground grits.

"How's the moonshine treating you this morning?" Sam said. He stared at David and tapped the paper. "The knife the FBI found in the fermentation tank is a sushikiri knife. They don't make those here in Kentucky, right?"

David was silent; he nodded, sipped on his coffee, then popped a whole beignet into his mouth and chewed.

They turned the Firebird off the highway just past a string of prefab condos and onto a thin, paved road. Sam was driving as David read from the precise map Perley had drawn the night before. A metal-gray Dodge with white doors and a flatbed flew past, it's dual exhausts rattling in the dust. They crossed over railroad tracks, beyond which a few abandoned and gutted pickup cabs sat among the weeds. A small brown shack with a slanted porch was tucked within the thickening trees, a faded cow skull above its door, and two white rusted metal chairs sitting vacant on its porch. The widely spaced oaks gave way to denser and denser woods, dead leaves draping the unkempt land.

The sun sliced out atop two large white oak posts and a cross beam spanning a long dirt drive. A solitary broad-winged hawk, caped in blacktopped wings, gawped at the Firebird as it turned into the drive. Sam looked at David to see if he felt it too—the hawk's warning—this feeling of trespassing on seemingly forbidden land.

The driveway was long, winding. The house startled them, springing up after a sharp bend. David had seen it in that old museum photograph, and yet it was not the same house at all. The center portion was of the original pen-logged construction, the unhewn logs reworked and saddle-notched, the original moss and mud caulk replaced with a hay and concrete paste.

Patches of epoxy covered spots of old rot, and the walls had been reinforced with new oak chinks. Side and back additions had been built as well as a second story with a Victorian dormer perched above. This new home dwarfed the dimensions of the original structure, but the cornstalks growing on either side and along the path still appeared larger than any David or Sam had ever seen.

"Get a load of those stalks!" David exclaimed. "I bet my Stillwater woman can bite through them with her teeth." He popped down the passenger visor and made eye contact with himself in the mirror, then flipped up one side of his collar. "Just to throw her off," he said and ran a hand through his wild, half-clean hair. Sam pulled the emergency break and turned the engine off.

She had been watching from the screen door, and yet Clara Stillwater did not come out to greet them on the porch. David sauntered up, his playful limbs confident as he hopped onto the elevated landing directly from the ground. Samuel, a few paces behind, utilized the warped stairs. The smell of hickory smoke hung in the air.

David looked eagerly through the screen, catching the diffused light of pale olive skin among the shadows—a quick swath of black hair. He rasped his knuckles on the doorframe.

"I see you have parked on my catchflies." Her voice was husky, serious.

David turned around, looked at the Firebird. Sure enough, sticky green foliage was smashed under the passenger-side front wheel.

"They must've, um, caught us," Sam said, suddenly embarrassed. "I will park somewhere else."

Clara opened the door. "What's done is done," she said, "I assume you two have already taken coffee this morning. Let's skip the chat and get into the fields." Only then did she step out onto the porch and reveal herself.

Tall and lean, Clara Stillwater had the stunning thoroughbred legs of her grandmother (David could tell despite the fact that they were downplayed by straight brown slacks). She wore a pale blue blouse tucked in at her trim waist, and a leather belt, beaded red and black. Her long black hair was combed straight behind her shoulders and precisely pinned at one ear.

David took a step back as Clara took a step out. Her eyes were not the piercing ice-fire of yellows and blue of her grandmother. They were brown, and their fierceness was somehow more intellectual than the untamed mystery of her elder kin. David focused on her lips, full and bowed. "So why the interest in corn?" she asked.

"Let's just call it the curiosity of whiskey science," David said, grinning like someone who is proud to believe his own lie.

She did not smile. Clara looked him over quickly up and down, and though her expression remained stern, her mouth betrayed a bit of pleasure as she noticed the partially flipped collar and his uneven shave. She then turned to Sam, stuck out a hand.

"I'm Clara Stillwater, ethnobiologist and president of the Bardstown Horticulture Society."

"It's a pleasure to meet you," Sam said. "Samuel Dugranval from the Institute of Fermentation, Distillation, and Maturation in New York." He nodded to the cornfield behind her. "That looks like Bloody Butcher, but those cobs are too small."

Clara smiled mischievously. "It is Bloody Butcher, at least in part. Come with me, and I'll tell you a little story." She moved past David without an introduction, fluidly stepping down from the porch.

"I'm David Dubehash," he said.

Clara did not seem to hear his words and kept looking into the field. "Yes, my grandmother told me about your visit last night. From the sound of it, she got you drunk."

David blushed slightly and grinned at the memory. "Your grandmother is quite remarkable," he said. "Full of spitfire and utterly beguiling. And she can sure hold her moonshine better than me."

"You sum her up well," Clara laughed. She stopped walking for a moment, her eyes met David's, and he felt her searching for something. He held her gaze. "My grandmother doesn't share that moonshine with just anyone, you know."

The two followed Clara from the house along a narrow path lined with yellow and red flowering Nasturtium plants. "They keep the aphids off the corn," Clara said, gesturing toward her feet. "And they have a wonderful peppery taste that us humans can enjoy." Here was a girl in her element, David observed, someone with an undeniable familiarity with the land, the crops, the critters, and who still managed to keep her hands impeccably clean.

Sam, meanwhile, was looking at the color of the dirt—a deep reddish-brown silt loam, on the drier side—that left him guessing as to whether this land was used continuously for corn or if other crops were rotated in. He opened his mouth with the beginnings of a question when Clara stopped.

"Here," she said, standing next to a plant that appeared no different than its surrounding brothers. She peeled back a section of husk, revealing the red meat, blood red, brilliantly so, the kernels small yet plump on the short, wide cob.

"Bloody Butcher originated in the early 1800s, maybe you know, when Native American corn mixed with the white settler's seeds," she explained. "This here corn was born shortly after, with the marriage of a Chickasaw woman and a traveling fur trader. Ostracized by her tribe for marrying this white man, and he an outcast by trade and circumstance, they had only her Redbird corn, his Bloody Butcher seed, and this fertile Kentucky ground to build a life upon."

Samuel reached out and touched the ear. *A corn born of marriage.* He felt far away from New York, out in this field in the deep woods, watching David pursue Clara. *The poor devil.*

"You must be interested in starch ratios," Clara said.

"Sure I am," Sam said. "I know that Bloody Butcher is composed of about 20 percent hard starch and 45 percent soft starch, which is very suitable for distilling. However I know nothing about this Redbird."

"Well Redbird is a popcorn," Clara said affectionately. "So the starch, as I assume you know, is much softer on the inside and is surrounded by a very hard exterior shell. This particular hybrid takes from the best of both corns, however, I'm afraid is best suited for family feeding, not for whiskey."

A flapping of wings was heard and two brown mourning doves rose, as if materializing from within the grain itself, silhouettes keeping low, banking toward the woods. David watched their synchronized flight.

He felt the calm range of this land and imagined what it would be like to live here. He could almost count the fence posts from here to Ohio.

Clara moved on in her effortless, knowing gait, following the direction of the birds into a shallow forest, through the patchwork shade, and emerging out the other side into another field of corn. She showed the men two separate fields, each isolated by woods to keep the strains from cross-pollinating, sharing them proudly, though with reserve, these grains of her world.

The first field was planted with short rows of Black Aztec corn, a sweet corn (though not sweet by modern standards) with kernels of a creamy white that Clara said would mature into a rich purple-black. Traditionally used for flour or dried and ground into livestock feed, Black Aztec was introduced into the United States seed trade in the 1860s from southern Mexico.

Not old enough, thought Sam. The corn used for Barclay's bourbon would have been growing in the United States decades earlier.

The second field was full of towering Hickory King, growing well above their heads. It was an old white field corn bearing bulbous, juicy kernels on narrow, seven-inch ears. Eight rows of corn striated each ear, not one more or one less, Clara pointed out—the trademark of authentic Hickory King. Used for corn nuts, hominy, and cornmeal, the kernels were widely spaced for easy shelling.

"It's great for grits," said Clara. "This variety has been growing in this soil for centuries, and soon after Columbus's voyages, it became a staple in Spain, Italy, France, and Egypt."

Sam was nodding, his disappointment apparent. This, too, was not what he was looking for—another plant for food and livestock, ancient but common. He knew its taste—a survivalist's corn. It could not have created that exquisite bourbon. They walked through more trees, sycamores, pin oak, green ash, and into rows of heirloom white flint.

"This was the corn that was brought by the natives to feed George Washington's troops when his army nearly starved. I'd recognize it anywhere," David said, eager to share.

"Oh, so you didn't sleep through my history class after all," Sam replied.

These fields, this lore, there was something to it—spirit and tradition overcoming hunger and strife. And yet it felt to Sam as if they were hitting a wall; *he* was hitting a wall. What were they discovering here? He felt like a tagalong on David's chase after another girl—and a girl who seemed to have already gotten the best of David.

No, Sam reminded himself, David had always sniffed out situations correctly in the past—let him be blinded by this ethnobiologist beauty. *Let him do the flirting*, Sam thought. *I'll do the thinking.* There was something to learn here, there must be, but what? Nothing they had seen fit the profile of the corn in his mind—that lingering mystery, a flash of grain, something almost sacred that he had tasted in Poughkeepsie. It was a step beyond the agriculture, the traditions, prospering corn. That bourbon had sprung from the culmination of a union of man and earth, beyond physical need, from a place of divine play, a place of art. Samuel thought of his mother, her meals made not just to nourish, but also infused with a love and respect for the flavors in things, everything prepared according to its nature and consumed in the proper order so as to be harmonious with the body and yield delight. He thought of the way his mother's eyes danced, a meal complete, sipping liquor as the evening wound down.

"Sam, you've got to check this out!" David was on his knees in the dirt. Sam felt like throwing something at him—an ear of corn, a rock. He breathed out.

"Arrowheads!" David yelled, "They're everywhere."

Clara was next to David, leaning in, looking at his upturned palms. In one, David held a long black triangular piece of flint, convex and heavy, and in the other, a smaller gray point, crude and light.

"Well, chief, the mystery's solved," Sam said.

David didn't hear him. "This larger one is definitely Shawnee," Clara was saying, "and the smaller was most likely from a transient tribe, one not accustomed to big Kentucky game. There were many battles here. The name Kentucky, you know, means 'dark and bloody ground.' The Indians fought for over four hundred years for this land, and in the end, the tribes all agreed that anyone could hunt here, but no man would be allowed to live in Kentucky."

Sam looked out into the field, searching for something he could not see, perhaps something that could not be found.

"Well, that's it, boys," Clara said, standing and wiping the dirt off her hands.

"What?" Sam asked, surprised. "What lies beyond those trees?" He pointed out to the field's edge.

"That's the end of our land." Clara looked at Samuel as though she were daring him to insult the size of her dominion. "But you're invited to dinner tonight at my grandmother's home." Clara shot David a glance. "Come on, I'll walk you two back to your fancy car."

CHAPTER SEVENTEEN

David was many places at once: in the cornfield gathering arrowheads with Clara, in the field behind his childhood house where summer beans would grow, and in the bed with the old ghost, his breath stale on David's neck. The stink of old age and cigar smoke dragged David back into the dark room. He was no longer dreaming, he knew, but was awake in the Talbott Inn, blinds pulled, groggy, confused, slightly love-struck, and sad for home.

In the Lincoln suite, Samuel, too, awoke from a nap. He had studied Parker's research most of the afternoon, through and through. then he went to sleep, angry at David for sleeping, and figuring he might as well nap also after finding nothing relevant in the confused files—save for a single exception. He had slept only briefly, without dreams, and woke up refreshed.

He rang David's room. "Fifteen minutes."

"Twenty," David replied.

In the lobby, beside the raccoon hats, bourbon candies, and the reception desk, Samuel stood rigidly in his gray suit and slim black tie. "David, it's been nearly thirty minutes," Sam shook his head. "And there is something else I want to talk to you about."

David was pulling a knit sweater on over his denim shirt. "What is it, Sammy dear?"

"Don't pull that Dubehash charm on me," Sam said. "I'm not Clara or Perley, which is what I want to talk to you about." Sam cleared his throat. "We learned nothing today. I don't intend to spend my life in Kentucky. I have a wife and a son." David felt Sam's loneliness. "Find out what they know," Sam went on. "And if they don't know anything more, let's move on. *Le cœur a ses raisons que la raison ne connaît point*, but you need your reason now, David."

They walked to Perley's, David leading the way, the sun retreating as it had when David took the same path the night before. At the front door, David rapped his knuckles, and they took in a scent of smoking game wafting from behind the house. Clara answered, beamed at David, and gave him a peck on the cheek.

"You look—"

"You're late," Clara said, still smiling.

"Stunning," Sam stepped up.

"Thank you, Mr. Dugranval," Clara said, and shook his hand.

"Where's the woman we came to see?" David asked, following Clara into the house.

"Oh, she's upstairs. The food is mostly on the table, and I've got quail on a spit out back."

David hungrily looked Clara over, starting at the white lace collar of her blouse, moving his gaze down to her trousers, the same from earlier that day, a bit of dried mud on the cuffs, and to her feet, delicate in leather sandals. His eyes took their time rising back up to her face to settle on those lips. "You have a bit of ash on your cheek," he said, and his hand went to rub it off.

"Must be from tending the meat." Clara pulled away capriciously. "This way."

She led them through the kitchen where David and Perley had drunk the moonshine, into a hall, and up an open staircase with a railing of cheap white-painted wood. It felt hollow to David's touch. It was hollow, Samuel knew.

Upstairs, in a candlelit room, a long table with five chairs was set, two places across from three. Next to Perley sat a man closer to Sam's age than Perley's. He was handsome and rugged, like a trapper might look, David thought. He rose to shake Sam and David's hands, introducing himself as "Roy. Roy McClannahan." Then he sat down beside Perley, who clasped his hand in hers and gave it a pat.

All along the lace table-runner were the foods Perley and Clara had prepared. Samuel felt a sudden pang of guilt for being so ill tempered and impatient earlier. This was a fine meal and these were good people.

"What a spread," David said.

"We grew the blue corn for those dumplings. And *that* is Nasturtium lemon butter," Perley said. "Your favorite, Roy," she smiled. "The water is juniper water with salt." She poured some into Roy and Sam's glasses.

"Where do you keep the blue corn growing?" Samuel asked. "We didn't see any at Clara's today."

"Maybe it's from another farm you own?" David offered.

"She must have overlooked showing you the few stalks of it we have," Perley said. "It's not a whole field," she added.

Clara came upstairs with a silver serving tray loaded with five plump quail, fire roasted and blackened, and set the tray down onto the table in a way that showed off her figure. Perley placed a long silver knife and a serving fork on the platter, and Rob stood to serve the birds.

"If there were a wagon train going West, and I were going West, I would want Clara to lead," Perley announced. "If I were not strong enough to lead myself, I mean, which I still am."

Clara did a mock bow like a man then sat down. "I wouldn't want to go West, anyhow, Grandma Perley. You get West and then what? Sand dunes and sea? Nothing beyond the horizon but water and Japan." She poured water into Sam's glass and then her own. "We already have enough Japs right here. And a lot of good they've done."

No one said a word. Roy laughed suddenly.

Perley shifted uncomfortably in her seat. "Samuel, I understand you and Woodrow Campbell were close. I'm so sorry." She corrected the drift of the conversation. "David, here, serve yourself some dumplings." Roy sat down.

"Yes, Woody was…" but Samuel decided not to go into it. "This meal looks and smells incredible," he said instead. "Perley, I'm very impressed. Clara, thank you also. And for showing us around the Stillwater land today." He took the dumplings from David and spooned several onto his plate. "Have either of you ladies by chance heard of a corn called Oaxacan Green? I was reviewing a colleague's notes today—well actually, I was looking over Parker Beam's research this afternoon and came across some interesting comments in a flatbed captain's diary about Oaxacan Green. Do you know anyone who grows this strain of corn?"

"It's an early-producer," Clara said. "Short stalks, small ears, slightly dented kernels that are a startling emerald green. I've only read—"

"Oh, so tonight will be all business?" Perley gave Sam a wink. "Oaxacan Green, if I'm not wrong, was grown by the Zapotec Indians in southern Mexico. I can't imagine it's ever been grown this far north." She looked at Roy who shrugged his wide shoulders. Clara looked at David. Perley saw, and David blushed.

"That's enough, you two," Perley scolded and raised a glass to the table. "Let's eat."

CHAPTER EIGHTEEN

Sam walked up to the front entrance of the Bardstown town hall, the tungsten glow filtering through the photocopied town bulletins taped to the doors, making him feel as if he were about to enter a late-night bingo convention. He could smell the warm blackberries of Perley's Kentucky Jam Cake wafting from the paper bag he held and hoped the Feds would have a fork.

Warmed with whiskey, mellowed by Kentucky hospitality, and feeling like he wanted to sleep, Sam leaned into the glass entrance door. It didn't move. He looked down—Pull. Sam pulled and walked a few off-kilter steps inside.

Agent Lefevre stood in a broad-leg stance in the hall. "Guess the doors are made differently back East," he said, arms across his chest, flexing and unflexing his jaw for a reason Sam did not care to comprehend.

"It's midnight, Lefevre, and I just left a table full of homemade pie and beautiful women. Whatever you called me here for, it better be as urgent as you made it seem."

"Come with me," Lefevre said, flicking his head and turning down the hall. Sam peeked into the bag as he followed, taking a big whiff of the pie.

The agent took Sam down a flight of linoleum steps and into a large basement hall full of folding tables covered in plastic, over which half a dozen or so men and women, all a bit bleary-eyed it seemed (or was Sam just projecting?), worked at various tasks. Numbered photos of the crime scene in plastic sheathes were spread over one table, several computer screens displaying various chemical graphs were set up on another, and farther in, a blood analysis machine emitted a low whir. A woman in white gloves and a lab coat leaned against it, sipping coffee, waiting for numbers to spit out.

Along the back wall, a table had had been cleared off. The only items remaining on its antiseptic surface were six long-stemmed tasting glasses full of amber liquid. "Nan! Really this is too much," said Sam. "I can't believe you, Lefevre. First you interrogate me and preach temperance like a Methodist. Now you're pulling out the fine china and inviting me over for a drink? Get someone else to do it." Sam turned, suddenly sobered with anger, and walked out.

Lefevre was on his heels. "Listen Dugranval—Samuel—please, wait."

Sam went out into the hall and began to climb the stairs. Lefevre stepped in front him.

"Samuel, you're right. I'm a teetotaler, yes, but let's start over fresh. I have great admiration for your work; in fact, I wish all drinkers were of your kind. You've done a lot for moderation, really. Everything is not so black and white."

Sam looked at him skeptically.

"My son," Lefevre went on, "is very passionate about whiskey. He's always talking about your school and your work, and he's always touting your online whiskey guide for Bonham's. I respect this passion of his, and I know you're one of the best in this field. My son wants to take your summer classes, and I support this."

Was Lefevre being sincere, or was he just using a good-cop routine to get what he wanted?

"I'll put it this way," Lefevre tried again. "This is important. We need to understand what's in that alcohol, and you're the only man who can help us. I know you'd never say no to a challenging whiskey tasting, especially when the stakes of the investigation are so high. We're talking about the murder of your friend."

Lefevre was right. Ego didn't matter here, and Sam wanted to find the murderer of Woody perhaps more than anyone else, save Beitris and Nate.

"All right," said Sam, "I'll do it, but I'm doing it for Woodrow, not for you." He turned around and walked back into the basement with Lefevre.

The liquid in the glasses on the table ranged from a light amber to a deep copper hue. Each had a sticker on its base labeled one through six.

"These are from a sample case we found at Four Roses," Lefevre said.

Sam looked again at the varying shades, then approached the glass farthest to the left. Lefevre was hovering over him, and Samuel turned, gave him an eye.

Lefevre backed off.

Samuel mentally stepped out of his surroundings, a cycle of breath, and stepped into a blank field of reception; an almost meditative state, free from the influences and prejudices from years of studying and tasting distillates—a clean space from which to approach the liquor, or rather, a space for it to approach him. He brought only the sensitivity of his senses, and the associations of his body and mind.

Sam picked up the glass and brought it to his nose. Inhaled, mouth open. Paused. Sniffed again. High citrus notes, yes. Oranges, candied lemon rind, and beneath? Sandalwood almost, burning Gingko, yes. A distinctive, familiar old-temple aroma.

"Japanese oak," Samuel murmured, and Lefevre's eyes lit up, though Sam was not looking.

Sam smelled each glass likewise, sniffing lightly, as the alcohol level was high and he did not want to "blind" his nose. He noticed subtle gradations of sweetness and that same exotic wood in each. In one, the high notes reminded him of baby aspirin, the sweet and soothing chewable remedy that helped Leo get to sleep; the pleasure of sloughing off responsibility, the certain late-night satisfaction of a day accomplished, a wife's face relaxed, the children gone to bed, and yet there was something else...

He began to taste.

Samuel went silent. There was something undefined, an experiment going on here, a delicacy of craft. He could smell and taste certain intricacies that were indicative of neither scotch nor bourbon—a broadening of the aroma and taste spectrums of whiskey as he knew it. *Precision, elegance*—Sam had no words exactly, only the silky, gliding mouth feel, and the movement of transformative flavors. Each glass seemingly pushed a different feature of the whiskey further: One tasted full of musk and oak, yet with an easy, sweet finish, a hint of stoned fruit. Another was bright and fruity, the citrus more of a tangerine on the tongue with hints of grass, green produce, and fresh grain. Corn was definitely the base for all—each sample an expression of a similar white dog—but this was not bourbon exactly. This reminded him of something...*what?*

A white room, a white table. A woman, pale, moving toward a transparent glass container. She cuts a single iris, its stem a length three times as long as the width of the vase. She positions the flower, her movements graceful, understated, carried out with a highly stylized etiquette.

The taste was changing. *Something denser, an intrigue, something dark, musky—not quite walnut, not quite truffle.*

Suntory Single Grain Whisky `Chita'—the workhorse of most Suntory blends! That's what Sam was reminded of, and yet, this was no beast of burden, *it's more of...more of...? Umeshu, yes, these had been rinsed in old Japanese plum brandy casks—that sweet finish could be nothing else.*

Samuel began to taste each glass again. There was order here, a method. The first glass was an expression that succeeded numbers two and five. Number three perhaps came next, and *oui*, number six was a culmination of the project, a creation fully realized. A new product, revolutionary even. Sam shuffled the glasses on the table, giddy with appreciation, arranging the samples in their true order, the sequencing of an unknown master distiller at play. He tasted them all again, smelled them all again, let the aromas rise retronasally in his throat, observed how they assimilated into a single note, and simultaneously he felt a warmth washing through his stomach, his body, his limbs.

Someone coughed. Sam turned around and was met with eyes, so many eyes. Everyone—the entire forensics team—stared at him. *How long had he been tasting?*

"Well?" said Lefevre.

Sam paused for a moment, the taste of the whiskeys lingering still. Could they read the excitement on his face? He tried to remain neutral. "Well it's not bourbon we're dealing with here, not exactly, I can tell you that." The agents were eager. Sam felt expectancy in their postures, their keenly cogent eyes. *They're desperate for a lead.* And yet he felt reluctant to tell too much. "These samples are corn whiskey, but they are much too refined and elegant to have been produced in Kentucky. Perhaps they were samples sent from overseas." *A marriage of bourbon and Japanese technique,* he did not say.

"I want to show you something," Lefevre said and made a gesture with his eyes that caused a chain reaction among the forensics team. Two younger-looking men hustled out and returned moments later carrying a wooden crate.

"This," Lefevre said, "is the container we found the samples in. It was tucked in a corner opposite the body, out of view behind one of the fermentation tanks."

Sam looked the crate over, simple plywood with black Hiragana characters printed on one side.

"Whiskey," said Sam. "All that box says is whiskey. It could be a left over crate from a number of places, or a new one made particularly for these samples. It doesn't matter. Its origins are Japanese, sure, but there are thousands of crates just like it all over Kentucky. Yesterday I saw one at a vegetable stand on the side of the road; it was full of Brussels sprouts."

Lefevre's face dropped slightly. "Surely you must taste the mark of a particular distiller in those bottles. Where did they come from? Kirin and Four Roses? Woodrow Campbell? Who?"

Samuel just shook his head. "Whoever made those was an excellent distiller and blender, that's for sure. A creative man or woman with a mastery of their craft, but who, I don't know."

"What aren't you telling me, Dugranval? You said 'Japanese oak' back there. What did you mean by Japanese oak?"

"I smelled an aroma that reminded me of Japanese oak, but that could be for a number of reasons. Someone was experimenting with wood is my guess. But again, that is only a guess, not a conclusion. Like I said, run the numbers if you want the facts."

"Let's take a walk," Lefevre replied.

The two men walked without speaking, back into the hallway, up the stairs, out the bulletin-covered door, and into the parking lot and brisk Kentucky night. Samuel carried the brown paper bag, the slice of Kentucky Jam pie now cold. His mind was racing with the implications of the new product development he had just tasted, yet his body was stiff. It was not that he wanted to withhold information from the FBI, no, it was that he was not sure yet what information he had. He needed to think. He needed to think without Lefevre's impatient investigation. But he also wanted to help; *Woody, poor Woody. Poor Beitris and Nate.* Samuel thought of the blood.

"Listen, Lefevre, I'll tell you what I do know."

They had stopped by the Firebird, its red body nearly black in the light, and its wheel wells, Sam noticed, were covered in dust.

"You'd be naive to think the killer is Japanese," Sam said bluntly.

Lefevre was taken aback. "What are you talking about?"

"The knife," Sam said. "A sushikiri knife is made for western chefs playing with sushi, chefs lacking Japanese craftsmanship. A Japanese killer would never use that knife. The Japanese are strict about the purpose of every knife. If it was a Japanese killer, they would have used an Kiritsuke knife, a samurai knife." Samuel caught his breath; he had not fully realized he had come to that conclusion before it came out of his mouth. "But it's more than that. I saw the photos of the body on my way in."

This last part caught Lefevre's attention. His eyebrows lifted ever so slightly, and he stared into Sam, reading his face, seeing that he was, without a doubt, telling the truth. "I'm listening," he said.

"I guarantee those cuts on the body are from a weapon with a double-edged blade, which is the western way of crafting a knife, the American way." Sam stopped.

Lefevre was quiet, serious, calculating something in his mind. "I wasn't going to tell you this," he said, and ran a finger along the hood of the car. He paused, then started again. "Well you were right about the tourists. We collected over two thousand different sets of prints in that fermentation house. And the chemical analysis of the tanks came out clean. No trace of blood in the vat with the knife. We don't have much to go on, I admit it, but I pulled you in here for the whiskey. What makes you such an expert on knives?"

Samuel smiled. "Well for one, my best friend is one of the finest knife makers in the world."

Lefevre scoffed.

"But he's French. My knowledge of Japanese knives comes from the owner of an amazing specialty knife store in New York. Korin, it's called. They have everything. I've been going there for over eight years now, I think. Fascinating place and well run."

Now Lefevre was the one smiling. "Swords are my passion. I've got a US Cavalry sword from 1864—regulation length, double-fullered blade, and a gorgeous curved edge. It's hanging in my study at home."

"The smell of iron always helps me think," Sam said.

Lefevre gave him a skeptical but friendly look. "You're a man of strange surprises, Dugranval." Then he looked at the car, smiled, made as if to say something, then changed his mind, nodded his head, and said something else. "It's late. I'll let you go. Thank you for coming in tonight. You've helped more than you know."

CHAPTER NINETEEN

M*ore than I know? But I don't know anything*, thought Sam. *Think. What is the significance of this Japanese style of bourbon? What was Four Roses doing with these samples? What does the murder of Woody have to do with it? What tree was I sniffing up back there in bingo hall?*

Sam's mind was a flurry of questions. The road was a blur. The Firebird stole through late-night Bardstown wheeled by a man on a blind mission heading toward the only solid thing he knew: Parker Beam. Samuel didn't care if he had to break the door down to rouse him—he needed to talk.

Red light impatience. Green. Sam turned onto Barton Street, the houses locked down for the night, their inhabitants threatened only by the dangers of sleep. He pulled into the Beam's driveway, the tires wet-sounding on the dry pavement, and Samuel noticed a single lamp burning inside.

His knock was quiet, nearly inaudible from within. But moments later, Parker was at the door in a long maroon shirt and matching pajama pants. A loose robe hung over his boney shoulders, bonier than yesterday's shoulders, it seemed.

"Parker. Thank God you're up."

"Can't sleep," he said, and motioned for Sam to come in.

Parker's study was lined with books, and on one wall, a glass display case showed varying samples of grain and corn. It smelled like fresh cigar smoke.

"Avo?" Sam asked.

"You know me too well," Parker replied. "Let me get you one." Parker opened the small humidor that sat atop his desk and pulled out a cigar for Sam. He clipped the tip and handed it over. Sam smelled it, sat down, put the cigar in his mouth, and was silent. Parker sat across from him in a matching worn-leather club chair, and the two stayed this way for several minutes, smoking, neither saying a word. Sam gathered his thoughts, let the taste of those samples sink in, and felt relieved to be in the company of a good friend. Parker was solemn and pensive. He looked like hell. A clock somewhere in the house chimed twice. It was 2:00 a.m.

"I just got back from town hall," Sam finally said. "The feds called me in to taste some whiskey samples they found at Four Roses."

Parker looked at him, surprised. "Samples of what?"

"That's just the thing," Sam said, "I'm not quite sure. They were beautiful and utterly odd. It seemed as if someone's developing a new corn-based whiskey in a Japanese style." Samuel went on to tell Parker the ranges of aromas and tastes he experienced. He spoke about the plum wash, the elegant feel, that old-temple uncannyness...for nearly a quarter of an hour. Sam described it all, going off on tangents of his knowledge—the specifics of Chita grain, the meticulousness and cleanliness of the distilleries he had visited several years ago in Japan, the way in which the Japanese had reappropriated Scottish techniques over the years and combined this knowledge with a few tricks of the Irish, French, and the Americans too, using the world's knowledge combined with the highest attention and control to advance the art of whiskey making into utterly modern realms.

"And let's not forget," Sam continued, "that it's not uncommon for blended Japanese whiskeys to have some young bourbon in them. I know your two-year-old Evan Williams goes in large shipments to Japan. Have you ever inquired about what it becomes?"

Parker leaned forward, about to answer Sam's question, when they heard a timid knock on the door. "It's me," Linda Beam said from the other side. "Can I come in?" She opened the door without waiting for a reply. "I'm sorry. I overheard your conversation." Her face was pallid, her eyes wide, and she stepped into the room wearing only a night-gown, her bare feet childlike. She looked vulnerable, afraid. "Sam," she said, "if you're looking for Japanese whiskey in Kentucky, there's something you should know."

Samuel looked at Parker, but the old man's expression revealed that he had no idea what his wife was about to say.

Linda sat down on the arm of Parker's chair and took his hand. "Several weeks ago, Beitris Campbell told me about a project Woody and Nate had been working on. They were attempting to engineer a new generation of whiskey. The project was big, and the boys were throwing themselves into it. They wouldn't tell Bea all the details, but she did know that the new product was supposed to revolutionize the way the world tasted and thought about corn. Bea was upset because her husband and son were isolating themselves and working many late nights on this new product. She was lonely. She wasn't even supposed to tell me about it—the project was expressly secret—but she needed to confide in someone."

"But Woody worked for Suntory. Why would the samples be with Kirin at Four Roses?" Parker gave words to the elephant in the room. "Was he selling his secrets to the other side?"

"That's what I'm afraid of," Linda said. "If he did, and Suntory found out, oh God. Those two companies have such a deep seated competition. If he betrayed them..." Linda went quiet. She looked at Parker, eyes wide with fear. "Parker, if they did that to Woody, who knows what they might to do Nate!"

CHAPTER TWENTY

The windows were curtainless, her skin flawless, but God had no mercy. David awoke in Clara's bed as elephant man—his eyes nearly swollen shut, his face a featureless and deranged bouquet of flesh. *Why now?* He pleaded silently.

David clenched his chest and crashed his face into the pillow, sucked in a breath. He looked over at her. Clara's back faced him, the homespun flax linen covers bunched about her waist, dark freckles forming a constellation across her spine. *Was she awake?* He watched her breathing. *No. Not yet.* He slipped out of bed and went into the bathroom. Shut the door, didn't want to look in the mirror, then looked in the mirror. *Shit.*

Where his eyes had been, David only saw tiny slits of lash. His nose was swollen to twice its normal size, red and blotchy. His upper lip had taken on the size and shape of a Polish kielbasa, and his cheeks seemed to have dissolved all the bones in his face.

David cursed again and felt a hot wave of frustration and shame.

Angioedema—it always got the best of him at the worst of times. A hereditary disease that made David's skin swell, its triggers were "idio-pathic," aka unknown, or idiotic in David's mind. His outbreaks were loosely correlated to allergen exposure and stress, but David could never predict when an attack would occur. *Had they used cinnamon to spice the quail?* David pried open one eye with a finger and thumb. *Or am I afraid of falling in love?* He snapped the eye shut. David's humor was coming back, slowly, dryly, and he began to accept the state of things as his image in the mirror looked more and more absurd. *Maybe I should just sneak out now and leave before she wakes. That's what I'll do.* But there was something about her, and despite his hideousness, David did not want to go. Last night, in bed, well the whiskey made it a bit of a blur, but he remembered a feeling of…a whole world in her. He couldn't quite put his finger on what it was, but he had surely felt something mystic, something allegorical as they made love. But he had also felt how she was blocked; she had walls built of a learned coyness, a predisposition to being defensively aloof. *She needs me*, David thought, *I can make her happy*. He studied his face again. *Oh God, no one needs this!*

David opened the medicine cabinet. Instead of the standard store-bought pharmaceuticals, cold creams beside nail clippers, and the like, David found a row of glass bottles with handwritten labels: valerian, lemon balm, skullcap, elder, burdock…He thought back to a botany class he had taken his second year of undergrad. *What herbs are good for swelling?* He heard Clara stir in the next room.

"What time is it?" she asked, sweet and lark-like.

"Um." David composed his voice. "Not sure. My phone is on the nightstand."

He heard some shuffling, her feet on the floor, a lighthearted yawn. David turned on the faucet and began to splash cold water on his face.

Clara walked over to the bathroom door and knocked.

He froze. "Uh, just a sec."

She opened the door anyway.

"Your face!" Clara let out a pinched gasp. In nearly the same instant, her wide eyes turned soft and a strong maternal instinct took over. With no fear and no fuss, she snatched up the bottle of elder, and shoved it into David's wet hands.

"Rub this on your skin and quick. I'll call a doctor." She turned, but David caught her by the wrist.

Clara looked up at his face, cringing a little, her cotton robe open at the neck revealing a swath of tan collarbone draped on one side by a perfect mess of hair.

David, naked, was trying to look as charming as the face-bloat would allow—a definitively pathetic attempt. "Don't worry. It's just something that happens to me," he said, and let out a stiff fake laugh. "Really it's no big deal."

"Mm hm." Clara's eyes widened, and she pushed her lips together in a cynical gesture of disbelief.

This time he laughed for real. *She's really worried*, he thought. "I know it looks bad," he said, "but really, I have some Cetirizine in my bag at the Old Talbott Inn. It usually clears this up quick. I'll just drive back—"

"Oh, you're not driving anywhere like that. I'll get it. You stay put." And like that, she was off, leaving the bathroom door ajar behind her. David watched her toss her robe to the floor and admired the line of her legs as she slid into those same brown slacks. She snatched up what looked like a man's work shirt and pulled its sleeves right-side out as she walked from the room still naked on top. David thought of her barging into the Old Talbott Inn demanding the room keys from the velour-suited brunette, Clara's lips still puffed with sleep, and no bra under that loose shirt.

He heard the engine of Clara's truck catch, followed by the roll of tires, and David felt a wave of relief at being alone, at knowing that no one would have to look at him. As soon as Clara returned, he would down the medicine, and all would be normal in time for lunch.

David rubbed some of the elder into his cheeks. It was cooling and smelled of dry grass. The swelling was uncomfortable, but not painful, not really, and David thought of other things, like coffee. He rinsed his hands on a towel and went into the bedroom in search of his pants. They were flung in a corner far from the bed, and he stepped into the legs awkwardly, his depth perception unreliable due to his swollen lids, causing him to sideways hop and knock into a willow basket full of academic journals. He replaced *The Kentucky Vegetable Growers Newsletter* on top of the stack and walked shirtless, barefoot, and groggy down the hallway into the living room. A coffee table made from a single oak slab—a smaller version of the table at Perley's—jabbed at his shins, and on the wall hung a leather tapestry depicting, in rough-hair needlepoint, a scene of three dark-tressed women standing in a field of corn. One woman carried a cauldron; another smoked from a long white pipe.

David passed through an archway at the far side of the living room into the kitchen and began the search for coffee. Again not a commercial product in sight. Atop the fridge sat jars of dried herbs and flowers: chamomile, rose hips, grape sage, colonial mint. There were brown leaves in a basket in one of the cupboards that smelled vaguely of licorice, and in the fridge, David found fresh butter, deep brown eggs, homemade jam—apricot perhaps—and a loaf of braided bread. In the freezer, next to a bottle of un-frozen liquid and in front of paper-wrapped meat, he found a tin can full of ground coffee beans.

As he took out the tin, David heard a loud thud followed by a scraping sound. He turned his head despite the fact that the sound had come from below his feet. *What the—?* He held still and listened, but heard nothing more.

He set a pot of water to boil on the stove to make the coffee cowboy-style, but the sound interrupted again—a rough scraping, like something being shoveled beneath the floorboards. He heard the creak of wood, then silence. *Raccoon? No, something bigger.*

David left the stove on high and traced his steps back to the living room. He had seen a door there that perhaps led to a basement, and sure enough, when he opened it, a narrow wooden staircase dropped into the dark.

He had to bend his head to keep from smacking the low door-frame, and he kept it bent going down. David ran his fingers along the wall, searching for a switch until a cold metal chain near slapped him in the eye. He yanked it, and a single bulb flickered then caught, spreading a dusty tungsten glow. The stairwell opened up onto a long rectangular room with irregular brick floors and low oak beams overhead. An expensive-looking steel shelving unit lined one wall, and embedded in the brick at the far end of the floor was wooden trap door, its hinges shiny and new.

The space was neatly kept and orderly as far as basements go. At eyelevel on the shelves were rows of jars, identical to those David had found in the kitchen. The collection of roots, herbs, leaves, and dried flowers was extensive, yet unlike the jars in the kitchen, these were not labeled, the meticulousness of their storage suggesting they were categorized by some other means. To the right of the impressive spice rack, the shelves bore trophies of basement miscellany worthy of the Oscar Getz: an unhung coat rack crafted from antlers and decorated with jade; a digging stick carved of bone with a worn leather handle; three earthen pots, asymmetrical and unused; and a stack of willow baskets, hand woven, like the one for periodicals upstairs. The usual basement suspects were also there: extension cords, a ladder, a grab-bag box full of batteries, phone cords, and electric knickknacks. There was a large settee cushion encased in plastic for a bench or piece of patio furniture David had not noticed outside, and on the lowest shelves rested heavy sacks of bulk dry goods: flour, or beans, or rice, or most likely ground corn.

David crouched and checked for signs of rodents or larger scavengers near the grain bags, but none were to be found. Everything was tightly sealed, and the floor looked as if it had been recently swept. David walked over to the trap door. *Perhaps an animal in the crawl space?* He tried the latch with no luck; it was locked.

David heard the sizzle of water spilling onto a gas flame. *The stove!* He bounded upstairs, turned the heat off, dumped a healthy portion of grounds into the boiling pot and lidded it with a plate. Atop the plate, David then stacked the braided bread from the fridge along with the dish of butter. He tucked the pot of jam under his arm, looped a mug with a spare finger, and headed out to the front porch. *What a house this woman keeps!* Everything in its place, an almost lab-like order that agreed with David, and he found himself shirtless and smiling with his bloated lips, the morning sun slanting onto the porch, illuminating a hideous face, but a happy man.

David looked out to the land and poured himself a cup of the brew. It was dark and gritty, satisfying in his teeth. He swished it around in his mouth, looked out at the driveway, swallowed, and chuckled at the smashed-up catchflies he and Samuel had flattened—was that only yesterday? Beyond the catchflies a dense thicket of primroses formed a natural yet deliberate hedge. Rising from behind or from within these primroses—David could not tell—was a thin but steady column of steam. *That's odd.*

David took a step off the porch to better see the source of the vapor, but at that same moment, Clara's baby blue, snub-nosed Ford came rattling up the drive.

"You think she's cookin' 'shine?" Sam asked in a mock Kentucky accent that wasn't half bad. He was sitting across from a now normal-looking David in the Proof restaurant, located in the 21c Hotel. A large red penguin looked over David's shoulder back at Sam. The hotel, in the heart of Louisville, was also a modern art gallery, and sculpted red penguins the size of bears were strategically placed throughout the lobby and restaurant as part of the collection.

"Either that or she's making witches brew," David said, somewhat disengaged and delayed.

"Neither would surprise me," Sam replied. "There's more to these Stillwater women than meets the eye, but don't get me wrong, there's plenty that meets the eye as well." He took a sip of water and paused. "I trust you did more than just look at Clara last night?"

David shot him a look that said "I don't want to talk about it." The expression was harsh, out of character. David was usually quiet after bedding a girl, bashful even, if it had been good—but he always reacted lightheartedly when Dugranval teased him, which Dugranval always did.

"Don't worry." Samuel studied the expression on David's face. "I won't say a thing about Clara to Mrs. B." He knew that wasn't what was bothering David, but Mrs. B. did have a tendency to intrude in David's affairs when it came to matters of the groin or heart. Sam pushed a little more. "Now don't you go falling in love, David. I need you in New York."

David was quiet for a moment. He fiddled with a fork on the table, his fingers testing out the sharplessness of each dull prong. "I had one of my Angio attacks this morning. It was a disaster."

Samuel laughed.

David leaned forward urgently. "It was fine at first. I mean, it was embarrassing and all of that, but she took it well. Or I thought she did. But as soon as I took my medicine, she started acting weird, like she couldn't wait for me to go. Said she had to prepare for the horse races today, something about the Horticulturist Society's booth, and she all but shoved me out. I didn't even finish my coffee."

"You poor thing." Samuel clucked his tongue. He squeezed his lips together condescendingly, but his eyes were sincere.

The food arrived at that moment. It allowed time for David to take a breath, and for Sam to take a proper visual and olfactory assessment of the dish: an assortment of house-made pâtés. He was pleased.

"She probably just needed to cool off a bit," Sam said after several bites, spreading pâté onto a second toast. "Girls like her are…like little horses."

"Colts?" David said. "Or fillies, technically."

"Colts," Sam repeated. "They are full of spirit, but they spook easily, especially if they sniff something serious coming their way." Sam raised an eyebrow at David.

David blushed.

"Well maybe I'll have a little conversation with Clara on your behalf," Sam was chiding again. "I was planning on dropping by the racetrack anyway. It's the opening day of the Fall Meet—everyone will be there, and I have some people I'd like to talk to. People who knew Woodrow better than me."

CHAPTER TWENTY ONE

David departed Churchill Downs flying solo for once and blasting *his* music—Waylon Jennings blared through the stock sound system. David was handling the machine with vigor. He was sneaking a cigarette, too, with the windows rolled down, the clean smell of earth and cool leaves flowing in. The tall oaks ran along the roadside, and thin, curved leaves he could not name rustled like flat cutouts of tiny bananas before him across the macadam.

David thought about Clara and Perley. What a family tradition they had—he remembered what Perley had said about corn and stories, and even though he was a chemist, it made so much sense. *They are the family I want to join stories with*, he suddenly realized, and he was surprised.

The music! How could it be that music didn't always sound this good? It was back. David was back, in love, though. Had he never been in love before? Was it time for him to review his sexual conduct, the scores of women whom he had charmed, and felt guilty for charming, and had felt the rush of experience with? No, it was time to move forward, and he had arrived.

David parked the Bird in the grass. He looked out at fields of corn, ready for harvest. He felt near home, and yet far from it. This was GMO corn. This was the GMO research facility where his friend, William, worked…as head chemist.

"Billy!" David shouted, playfully kicking out one leg in his stride down the hall. He wore the wrinkled clothes of the day before, moving through the stringent lab of vinyl floors, whitewashed stucco walls, and square windows that did not open. David looked into the offices and labs of various other chemists, all working for William. The facility was astringent, but he smelled Clara and tobacco on himself.

"Dubehash," William Michel called, cool in a lab coat, a white package of cigarettes in the chest pocket, expensive loafers standing out against the white of his pants. The two shook hands and William grabbed David's arm below the elbow with affection. William was tall, taller than David, and his dull gray eyes flickered with intellect. His mouth and the area around his eyes contorted happily. "Good to see you, old friend."

William must be pulling in six figures, David guessed. "You look the same as ever," he lied, and shook William's hand. The two men stood, as odd friends do, having no idea what to say.

"Let me show you around," William finally offered.

"Hell, that'd be a start."

They toured the building, then stepped out into the sunlight to look at the fields and smoke. David was exhausted, not having slept much the night before, and the cigarettes didn't help. "So, you're working for the enemy camp," he said, taking a drag. "GMO?"

"Welcome to the real world, David. We can't all be working in NYC in a dream job, pulling in women left and right. Which you *are* doing. Tell me you are?" William considered something, then added, "But I bet you're not pulling down the kind of mares I grab here. Only downside is, I have to live in Kentucky. But you know what they say, 'Kentucky, where the horses are beautiful and the women are fast.'"

"Actually I did meet a woman here. I think I'm falling in love." David looked seriously into the field. "Maybe I'll move in," he said. "Be like old times." He turned to face William. "Now explain to me, using chemistry, why you really think it's safe to splice *Rattus norvegicus* DNA into soybeans? Or let's just use the regular terms—rats! Jellyfish into corn? Or bovine genes into tobacco? Or human genes into rice? Chickens into corn, along with Hepatitis B?"

"You're really going to start this right now?"

"Come on and defend yourself, Billy," David jabbed. "Tell me how you sleep at night."

"Well, David, this is the way of the future. It may be possible for us to take a field of earth and use it to cure cancer, or solve the energy crisis, or the hunger problem. The Earth's getting overcrowded, and we're running out of resources. We know we can grow corn that produces a higher yield, of course." William kicked an old apple core on the ground. "And we can make pest-resistant—hell, who am I kidding—nearly pest-proof crops, so that's a start. We can make rice with more iron and protein for the Africans starving over there. Corn that glows in the dark." William was getting excited. "Well who knows what that will give us someday. This is the forefront of chemistry, David. You know this. And don't give me that shit about it ruining all the non-GMO crops or how all the seeds self-destruct and make farmers dependent on Monsanto, or Dupont, or any of us GMO suppliers. That can all be undone. The original seeds of almost every edible species are being protected, and we can figure out how to make GMO varieties that won't overtake their non-GMO brother and sister crops." William stomped out his cigarette. "This stuff is already in the world. It can't be ignored. It's the future and it's the present. Europe will come along. Africa loves it. It's not so black and white, David."

"And it's not clear what *it* will do," David said, taking the charge. "We know it is displacing all the non-GMO crops. Hell, the only way to protect a crop is to have it surrounded by forests." David thought of Clara, her genius. "And the people you are working for, who stuff your throat with cash, they are taking the farms away from little guys who don't buy their seeds. They are making terminator seeds so that the African farmers have to pay for the seeds every year—all the farmers have to pay. Soon as they can't, they go into debt, and from there, they lose everything. Hell, when I was a boy on our farm, we saved our own. We used our seeds year after year when we collected from the past year's crop. It's the human way. And those African GMO farmers' neighbors, who don't buy the seeds, they get their crops infected by your GMO crops, and they can't harvest their own seeds because their crops have mutated. Then they have to take out loans to buy

GMO seed and pesticides because the seeds you are selling them are pest-proof only for certain pests, and the genes that have adapted for millions of years to resist the local threats have been erased. These GMO crops have no history, no story, no tradition, no life source. They are death made to live. Don't kid yourself, William. You've become the worst type of chemist. The worst."

"Um." William backed down. "I was going to ask you over for supper—"

"You son of a gun!" David laughed. "Give me another smoke. The tobacco around here isn't GMO is it?"

William chuckled halfheartedly and handed David a cigarette. "This one's part tobacco, part filet mignon." He paused, began to pull out another cigarette, but slipped it back into the pack. "To be honest, many people 'round here share your opinions. I'm not the most popular guy in town." He looked up and pointed. "See that gristmill over there? We're lucky it's still intact. One of our employees attempted to sabotage it last year as a protest to GMO. Threw rocks in with the corn to start a 'natural' fire. Insurance company figured it out. Unfortunately the perp was from a very respected family in the area, so charges were never filed—that's Kentucky for you."

David shrugged and stared into the field.

"Anyhow, have a meal with an old friend?"

"Hell," David said, "why not?"

The house where William lived with his mother was covered with a discolored, rolled metal roof that bore down on a large central turret and several two-story porches with peeling paint. In the yard, behind iron-gate fencing, cylinders from cat food cans were rusting, and on the porch, cats swarmed: feral and domestic, obese and skeletal, mean and scared—there were tabbies, calicos, bobtails, bangles, blacks—some curved and hissing, others sleeping through the late striations of dusk.

David was tired. He knew cats from the farm days, unless cats had changed too (it seemed everything was changing), but David had no idea what to make of William's home. *Infestation. Last dance. Cat-hoarder's Kentucky estate?*

It was depressing standing there, waiting for William in the last of the orange light. William was behind the wheel of a white dual-side exhaust F350, with monster tires and tinted windows, talking into a phone. David saw what looked like the same gray and white flatbed from the day before tear up the street. He heard the tires catch, screech, and a backfire. *Was he being followed? By who?* On the porch, a cat swiped another cat near its eye.

"David," William said as he approached his old friend, having quit the truck. "Thanks for coming out. And, um, just be calm around my mother, will you? She's grown funny." William made a face. "Well, come in."

In was better than out.

Inside the house was well furnished and clean. The smell was curious—a warm appetizing aroma beneath cigarette stink.

"Kentucky Burgoo," William said. "Find yourself a drink while I change clothes." William left David standing in the large foyer, slipping out of his shoes. David could hear the cats outside—and could imagine the feeling of coming home to this place. Beneath the food and cigarettes, it smelled of cheap-treated materials, polymers, and compressed particles.

Somewhere on the other side of the open kitchen, William's mother coughed. A wet and dry, clinging, phlegmy sound. A large-woman's smoker's cough. He smelled a cigarette. He went through the kitchen and into the sitting room, where the folds of something enormous overhung its seat. She was facing away, but bits of thin curls could be seen from the edges of the straight-back chair. A large leg hung to one side, in sweats, and Dave saw the columnar folds of her cotton shirt. For whatever she had become, for this long-past object of maternity, David blamed the cats.

Dinner was terse. They ate. They passed. She coughed. Didn't David have a date with Clara tonight? *No.* David tried not to stare at the woman, his friend's mother. In New York, you never had to eat in a home with a friend's mother it seemed. Everyone's mother was somewhere else, or at least, different from a mother in their New York ways. Everyone knew enough to be ashamed, if they were to be ashamed, and to cover it with something. Everyone had something they were *talking* about. She ate. The burgoo was tasty, and David was hungry. David tried not to look at William. He didn't drink.

"So, David, tell us about this local woman you are falling in love with," William finally said, as the plates became emptied. It sounded so strange, the way William said it. David wanted to let the cats in, to let himself out, to get back to the day now lost, to get back to last night by seeing Clara again.

"Well, William. Let's see—"

He began by telling about the angel's kiss of her lips, how God had cut a notch there and what it was like to look at a mouth like that. He told of her wild mane, her hair when she woke. Then he naturally started telling the story of his attack that morning, and the mother actually laughed when David described his features, and Clara seeing him in such a state...but as soon as he'd said Clara, the mother shrieked.

She stepped down on the lone inside cat's tail. The cat was below the table; David had somehow not noticed it. The cat yowled and cut its claws into the mother's leg. She rousted up out of her chair and nearly fell backward. "That woman," the mother said, pulling the cat off her leg. There were nicks of blood through her sweats. "She tried to burn the lab down!" she yelled. "That's Clara Stillwater!" The mother shot David a hateful look. "I hate that woman!"

"Um, David," William said, making a motion to stand up, but stopping short. "Was it really Clara Stillwater you slept with last night?"

"Maybe I should go," David said awkwardly.

"Yes, David, you better leave," she said. "And you tell that woman—" the mother wheezed and coughed.

"Here, let me walk you out," William said before his mother could finish. Outside he explained what had taken place. How Clara had gotten the job. How he had Clara over for dinner a few times, and how his mother had decided William should try to marry her.

"I'm sorry about my mother. But really, she's right. That woman tried to sabotage the lab," William said. He stuck out a hand for David to shake.

"Good night, William, and thanks for the food," David said, shaking the hand, then quickly turning and walking through the cats to the Firebird. He climbed in and turned the engine. His stomach was in knots. Clara was a good woman. David was sure. He thought of the trap door in her basement with the deadbolt. Well he was mostly sure. He thought about the noises he had heard that morning. How could that steam have been from 'shine when Clara was asleep all night beside him? He needed to get there and have a look, if only for some peace of mind. David pushed the Firebird into third gear and was flying back toward the old Stillwater homestead, hoping against hope he wouldn't find anything, and that somehow he would be able to see her tonight.

CHAPTER TWENTY TWO

S am thought about Woody. *He should be here now.* The twin spires rose from the grandstands at Churchill Downs into a weightless sky splotched with clouds. Sam walked from the Longfield parking lot where David had dropped him and approached the spires behind the western section of the grandstand. A thicket of chatter rose from the crowd. Sam banked left under blazing maple trees and came round the other side to the valet parking post in front of the clubhouse. A woman in loose blue slacks that stopped short at midcalf stepped out from a grill-heavy Cadillac and parted with her keys. A younger woman in a smart black dress and white jacket got out behind her, and Sam hung back to let them enter the building first.

Faces were everywhere, many red with drink. Sam was sure he would run into someone he knew, and to avoid small talk before it was absolutely necessary, he quickly veered toward the steps and stuck close to the white wood paneled wall in the stairwell. His heart rate rose as he climbed to the fifth floor.

The private suite was reserved under Woodrow Campbell's name. There had not been time to cancel the booking, so Nathaniel Campbell had decided to go ahead with the annual Fall Meet gathering his father had planned. *Dad would have wanted it this way.*

Sam gave his name to a young usher in a green sports coat and entered a carpeted corridor. The door to Campbell's suite was cracked open a fraction of an inch, the voices coming out of the room distinctively less jovial than in years past. Samuel silently entered, trying not to remember the last time he had been here while also trying not to bring much attention to himself, but his phone went off. Enough heads turned to announce his arrival to all. It was a text message from Renoux.

"Hidden Balisong. Blade on track concealed by false-blade that is second handle. To release: press on dark spot in thuya burl while pulling left side of frame back and gripping with index finger at choil…"

Ingenious, Sam thought, and his mouth loosened into an almost-smile despite the somber mood. Well at least it was a distraction. He started to reach for the knife, but then thought better of it and dropped his hand at his side. Several dozen men and women stood around the plush room in various poses of gravity and feigned festivity, some smacking on cured meats with jams and chutneys, sweet and hot pickles, barbecue shrimp, buttered asparagus, and other items from the lavish (yet provincial, in Sam's mind) buffet. No one was sitting down on the leather sofa or upholstered armchairs, but everyone held a drink.

Sam walked over to the bar where a clean-shaven local boy in a black bowtie gave him the only real smile in the room. "What are you mixing?"

"Russian Caravan," the chap replied. "It's the official drink of this year's first Fall Meet."

Samuel knew the drink well, as it was invented in a contest between patrons several years back at his regular lower-Manhattan haunt, The Brandy Library. "Perhaps this place isn't as provincial as I thought," he said to the bartender and nodded his head in appreciation as he took the glass.

Samuel turned toward the windows and had a long look at the track. The yellow-brown dirt was smooth and clean, but there was a palpable tension in the collective posture of the crowd. A race was about to start. Sam could hear bets being placed halfheartedly across the room, and beyond the glass, the jittery yapping of announcers on loud speakers in the stands. From a stranger's perspective, this would seem a glorious day for a race. The sun was out, a cool autumn dryness was fresh in the air, but Sam was no stranger here. A foreigner, perhaps, but he knew the ins and outs of this track, this suite, and the whiskey women and men who knocked back their highballs here. And yet, as Sam had learned over the past few days, there was also much that he did not know, too much. And it had cost a life. The smoky cocktail—dark and complex on the tongue despite the light elderflower and honey notes on the nose—was uncannily apropos.

He spotted Nathaniel across the room talking to a short man in a tan-and-pink-striped suit with a matching tan tie. Nate's boyish face was flushed, but there was a tightness to his jaw and a tension in his forehead that made the boyishness suspect. Here was a man. Sam's heart dropped at the sight of him.

Sam eased his way across the room, giving a woman he recognized as an assistant to Woodrow a slight tilt of the head in lieu of a hello. He stepped into the circle of conversation with the tan-suited man.

"So I told him to go piss up a rope," the suit was saying.

Nathaniel grimaced a little.

Samuel put a hand on Nathaniel's shoulder, pinched the stiff muscles there. "Your glass is empty, Nate. Come on, let's get you another." Sam guided Nathaniel to the bar, but when they got there, Nate said he was fine and didn't need another drink. Sam ordered a second for himself. "Well then, let us go take some air."

Without explanation to the tan suit, the two men walked out, Sam holding his drink low and slightly behind his leg as they passed the green jacket ticket boy. They stepped into an open elevator. Nathaniel pressed the button for level three. Sam let out a breath. "There's no easy way to say this," he started, "but I can tell there's a lot you're not telling me. Nate, I can read it in your eyes."

The announcer was piped into the elevator—a jumpy British slant reeling off the win odds from the tote board as the last of the spectators scrambled to wager before the bell. "Haley's Comet still the favorite to win with seven to two at three minutes thirty to post, Windago with a Raise a Native sire line at three to one, Naughty New Yorker is stacking up a healthy seven to one…"

Nathaniel looked sharply at Sam. "My money's on Graceland," he said.

"Three minutes to post. Get your bets in."

"Listen, I—" The elevator doors opened onto the Turf Club and a clamor of speculative noise and shifting feet. They stepped out onto a carpet of yellows and reds spreading across the room. A plump woman in a blackrose hat and a geometrically loud dress leaned back in a chair, laughing. A balding white-haired dignitary-type bit on his thumb and mumbled to himself as he read the odds on an overhead LCD.

"Can we go somewhere, *euh*...quieter?" Sam asked.

A vested waiter passed with a tray of jingling drinks.

"After the first race," Nate said.

"Of course, of course."

They squeezed their way across the room, Sam recognizing many faces, Nathaniel recognizing more, and both deterring their eyes from the wave of empathetic looks laced with, perhaps, a touch of fear that followed Nathaniel's aura of grief. The young man rolled his shoulders back and buttoned his jacket, *as if that button had the power to keep him safe from the world,* Sam thought.

Several steps down, the lower level of the dining area butted up against windows overlooking the track. Nathaniel moved past the broad back of a man with a diamond studded ear—*an NFL pro?*—and found a space in front of the glass. Sam remained half a step behind, hands in pockets, looking between bodies at the track.

"They're in the gate." The announcer was skittish. "And they're off!"

The room went quiet for a moment, and then burst into yells. "Go, go!"

"Dr. Pepper. Push out, baby, move," someone behind Sam yelled.

Sam looked intently at Nate, who stared out at the track, nose near the glass, lips pressed, a fist unconsciously half-raised—his posture broken off, frozen.

"Windago just loping along here, breezing through the first furlong, Windago leading by three, Heart Stealer in second, waltzing through the opening quarter mile. Naughty New Yorker moves up in the field to second as Windago continues to run off the rail in a relaxed position. Room on the inside for Naughty New Yorker..."

The horses flew by.

"He's on the outside of the other," someone said.

"Windago leads them under the twin spires with a circuit to go. Naughty New Yorker making ground on the inside, Heart Stealer next, followed by Sheer Trouble in fourth, then Graceland toward the outside together with Velvet Coat…"

The horses were gone, disappeared for a moment behind the infield, then visible again, a fury of flanks along the backstretch.

"Toward the halfway, Graceland moving up to fourth, forty-six seconds left, toward the half on the sharp end, it's Dr. Pepper making a move from behind six lengths back. Windago still in the lead, Naughty New Yorker with an early run now, Naughty New Yorker moving up to take that leader, Windago going fast, but nowhere to go!"

"Get through, get through!" A blonde in delicate silk shrieked and jumped to her feet. Sam watched the fit of tendons in her neck and suddenly felt very alone. He looked at Nate, who was completely still.

"Heart Stealer looking for room. They are homeward bound now. Naughty New Yorker making some headway, and Velvet Coat opens up!" The noise behind and in front of the glass, out the TVs, and through the loudspeakers leaped into an ear-buzzing roar. "Velvet Coat kicks into high gear on the final furlong, moving from behind, he takes Naughty New Yorker, passes right on by Windago, Velvet Coat has taken over by two lengths!" The announcer's voice rose to a shrill. "Velvet Coat flashing home, and it's all Velvet Coat! Velvet Coat wins the opening race of…"

Nathaniel abruptly turned around. "Let's get out of here."

It was quiet in the truck. Samuel and Nathaniel sat in the cab of Nathaniel's dark green GMC pickup, parked near gate six, out behind the stable offices at Churchill Downs. "Butch Lehr, the track super, ever meet him?" Nate asked and took a sip of Elijah Craig 18 from his flask.

Sam shook his head. "No. Hey, do you remember when you over-reduced that batch, and nearly failed my summer course at IFDM?"

Nathaniel grinned, but did not laugh, "Has it really been four years?" He handed over the flask.

"Almost five now. Poor Mrs. B. nearly lost her lunch all over the lab."

"Never made that mistake again," said Nate.

There was a silence.

"Listen, I..." Sam paused. "Nate, I have to ask you something. It's just eating me up."

Nathaniel's chest seemed to fill up with something heavier than air. He looked at Sam. Waited.

"Last night, I heard that you and your father were working on a secret recipe, which I assume was funded by Suntory, but what I just can't seem to get my head around is that you two would then be working for the competition, Kirin, at Four Roses."

Nathaniel's chest dropped. Sam handed him the flask, and he took a big long gulp. "Japanese Oak," Nathaniel said.

Samuel's eyes flashed.

"Remember several years back when my father spent six months working for Suntory at Hakushu? Well when he returned, he wouldn't stop talkin' about how much he was in love with the sophistication in the distilling process of Japanese whiskey, how gorgeous their methods were, especially on the high proof distillation. You know all of this." Nathaniel fiddled with a sticker on the dash. "But what you don't know is at that time, I was having a bit of a crisis. I needed to go out on my own. I needed to crown my career, something that would perpetuate our family name. Something worthy," he almost whispered the last part. "And I thought if my father could help me translate these Japanese methods into a Kentucky corn recipe, well, Sam..." Nathaniel trailed off, his eyes going distant again. He swallowed hard.

Sam didn't know what to do with his body. He wanted to hug Nathaniel, wanted to let him just cry, but it would be awkward leaning over in the truck. Sam nodded his head. "Go on, Nate."

Nathaniel exhaled and gnawed on the corner of his lower lip. "So he did. My father helped me. Outside of Suntory and in secret, we created a blend of two distinct traditions. We made a pretty damn fine whiskey that's in a category all of its own. You should taste it, Sam."

Perhaps I already have, Sam thought. "Send some over to me tonight," he said.

Nathaniel's face was flushed. He locked eyes with Sam. "The product is good. Beyond good. It's…it's gonna change the way things are done. And well, about two months ago, we were finally ready to start commercializing. We had everything lined up. But Suntory found out, and they were pissed that dad was working on a new product without their consent. Breach of contract. Sent my father a termination letter and everything. He hadn't told anyone, not even mom. He was trying to smooth things out. I mean, I understand that Suntory was angry. I just didn't think they would go this far."

CHAPTER TWENTY THREE

The moon rose behind the forest of the old Stillwater homestead. David had parked the Firebird along the catchflies, despite having thought the entire drive over that he would park off the gravel road before the long drive and cover the Firebird with tree limbs like he'd seen done in a film. The fantasy was just dumb logic he used to get himself to the house. *What am I doing?* But somehow David felt Clara would laugh about this. And he had to find out about her if she was hiding something. What would Sam say? Would he understand?

David checked to see if there were any lights coming from inside the house. He watched the dark glass under the lattice perch, but there was nothing he could see. The additions to the old home in this light seemed more in keeping with the photograph at the Getz. Something felt right about being here, though he sensed he was being watched, and the feeling grew.

The quiet chirping night broke with the screech of a barn owl, its claws tucked into its underbelly, as it flew over David in a white flash. The animal world knew he was here. David came around the far wall of the newest wing of Clara's home, seeing how the new paneling contrasted with moss growing up the cracked old foundation and the peeling paint off the wood. *Everyone knows everything. She'll know,* David told himself and felt like a cheat.

There was something he wasn't thinking of. What did he keep sensing about this place? The land was nearly square, cleared for a good stretch, then younger trees grew, beyond which sat the fields and the old forest. *This is the only one way to find out,* he decided.

He smelled the leaves, the spicy aroma of the nasturtiums and the tang of pine mixed with the deep-nose scent of brewing hooch. Rain was coming. She *was* brewing hooch, and *he* didn't belong here. *It's part of her allure. Stillwater moonshine.* David thought about those drinks he had at Perley's. *They know their stuff.*

He stepped lightly to keep from tracking deep in the soil, and came around the back of the house where thick cornstalks stood, their ears bent toward the blackness beyond. A crescent orange moon crested the tree line. It made him think of a Stillwater ancestor rising with a rim of a lamp, watching. *Am I trying to ruin my luck with Clara?*

David had left the bathroom window latch turned open that morning, and he pushed up on the window to see if was still unlocked. The pane moved, and bracing the wall, he pushed the glass completely up, catching a long splinter and cursing as he pulled it out with his teeth. His blood smeared a little on the sill.

Half into the window, David worked one shoe off with the other foot and the other shoe with a socked toe. He would leave the way he came in, and his shoes wouldn't track in dirt. *She'll never know I was here,* he hoped.

He passed through the dark house and into the kitchen. His coffee mug was still in the sink, and his heart sank a little. He entered the basement stairwell, and this time knew where the light chain was, but did not pull it. The walls felt gritty as he groped his way down and to the landing. He could scarcely make out the trap door. It was open, he realized. And the lock was gone.

He crept down the cracked poured steps that led below the trap door, smelling a rank smell of mold and dirty clothes. It was even darker in this sub-basement, but David could make out a faint light ahead. He listened for Clara's truck but all he could hear was his own breathing. The ceiling lowered on a slant, and he had to crouch down and squat, moving awkwardly through the black. At the end of the cramped passage, the room opened up, and a bare bulb, its filament burning low, shone on a faded brown, stacked washer and dryer.

A rope was strung between two eyehooks on connecting walls making a diagonal cross-section from which clothes hung, drying. And then he saw it: a soft-copper still, modern in make, like an immense cocktail shaker with a serpentine coil twisting down around the top third of the shaker to where the vapor cone handles lay, the entire rig set upon a glowing stone furnace. He could hear the mash swirl and churn inside releasing a bready, familiar scent. David listened to the whispers through the worm entering the carboy jug. *What was that?* He thought he heard something other than the hiss and churn of the mash.

David looked at the clothes hanging on the rope, fastened with old one-piece clothespins. A pair of worn-out overalls. A white tank top, stretched out where a large belly would be. There were men's socks and a flannel coat. The tank top held faint yellow stains. The overalls were also stained, their denim splotched with brown, which had been washed and rubbed as if against a rock. The scent of the room was sourly masculine, overpowering and mildewy under the scent of the cooking moonshine. David heard something again but could not decipher where the sound came from. He froze. He looked all around. There was nothing. He had to think. "Hello?" David called out. "Hello, I'm a friend of Clara's." Something moved behind him, fast, and struck the back of his head. David's vision tunneled through a dark passage into blackness.

CHAPTER TWENTY FOUR

Sam needed to piss. Two, maybe three, more races had come and passed as he and Nat had nursed the flask dry. The hum of the crowd in the grandstand registered low and far off, a buzz within a buzz in Sam's ears as he walked the back-lot near gate six at Churchill Downs. Nat had headed home in his truck, said he couldn't stand the thought of going back inside, and Sam couldn't blame him. *Couldn't help him either,* this boy turned man by so much loss. Sam kicked a plastic cup someone had dropped on the ground. It didn't go very far.

Sam, too, had no desire to go back into that clubhouse, to make nice to the tan-suited man, to the secretary without a boss, to pretend the world had not gone mad. Nathaniel was lucky in one sense at least: he was close enough to home to go there now. Sam had only the Talbott Inn, and his phone, the disembodied voice of Lydia at the end of the line, the background noise of his son...he wanted to call Lydia now. Just as soon as he found a place to piss.

Sam tried the door to the maintenance building—desperate for a bathroom without a line—and found it unlocked. The steel peg echoed off the concrete in a hollow whine as Sam pulled the door open and stepped in. "Hello?" No answer. A wide hanger-like space opened up before him, the sharp metal teeth of a Horsemen's Track Conditioner shining blue in the dim light. Beside the beast was a bright orange three-point hitch track harrow, and on the floor, a detached brass spray nozzle from a water truck.

The overheads were off, save a pulsing energy-efficient glow from a hallway to Sam's right. Sam quickstepped it to the hall, passing a closed glass door with Venetian blinds barricading what he assumed was an office within. The next door was on a swing-hinge and looked bathroom-like enough. Sam went in.

One of the two stalls was occupied, its tenant flushing as Sam made a beeline for the urinal. An acne-faced young man in coveralls came out, his skin that pink that never tans. He gave Sam a scowl and left without washing his hands. Sam unzipped. *Ah, the simple pleasure of a bodily need fulfilled.* It was one of those endless pisses. How much had he drunk? Sam enjoyed the relief and let his mind wander. He thought of Scotland and his repeated trips to the loo there, having drank so much beer with his single-malt-making friends. *It's like they didn't trust the water and made up for it by drinking an excess of beer.*

The bathroom door opened behind him, and Sam heard the steps of heavy boots. He caught a glimpse of the acne-faced kid again, and someone else, a bearded and bulky man, followed by a sharp pain and Sam's legs giving out as he was hit behind the knees with a metal rod. His confused French face crashed into the porcelain urinal, his hands too slow to catch him—*damn whiskey*—but Sam regained his reflexes quick and spun to face his aggressors. A boot kicked toward his face, but Sam deflected it with a fast arm. A third man was in the bathroom now, older looking, his head shaved bald, a black fire shining in his eyes. The bearded man grabbed Sam under the arm and hoisted him up. Sam twisted around, slipping out of his grip and gave him a hard kick on the shin. Sam made a move for his knife, but the acne-faced kid hit him hard in the back, sending him hurling into the bald guy, who trapped him in a bear hug while the other two pulled Sam's arms back and bound his wrists with a zip tie.

"What are you, the redneck police?" Sam snarled. He kneed the bald guy in the thigh, hard, which made him yelp in pain then retaliate with a shoulder-backed punch to Sam's face.

"Foreigners ain't got no rights in Kentucky," the acne-faced kid said.

The three men dragged Sam out of the track maintenance building to a dually flatbed that had been spray-painted gray. They threw Sam onto the flatbed, and the three of them hoisted a half-ton bag of fertilizer onto his lap. Dead weight in place, they then went to work tying up Sam's legs.

They drove for what seemed like hours, the engine deafening, every bump in the road sending shooting pains up Samuel's legs and into his spine. His head throbbed, his buzz was entirely gone, and the cuffs were bloodying up his wrists. The fertilizer bag was causing the grooves in the bed of the truck to bruise his entire backside, and it obscured all but a patch of sky from view. Sam managed to crane his neck and make out a blur of trees whizzing past. At one point, a road sign flashed by—*Highway 62?* He couldn't be sure. A rush of cooler air came upon him, the sound of the road changed as if they were going over water, and then an unmistakable smell: mash cooling in slop ponds. A distillery was near.

The truck veered left and would have thrown Sam had he not been pinned by the shit. They hit dirt, Sam's organs banging against each other, dust filling the air. The truck stopped.

Doors slammed, there was a crunching of dirt underfoot, and the bald man was staring down at Sam with those black eyes, looking like he was going to spit. "Have a nice ride, Frenchy?"

The boys climbed onto the back of the truck, hauled the bag off of Sam's legs, and dragged him. He was pulled up and left to stand. He felt a tingling in his limbs, a rush of blood to the brain, and he pitched forward to the ground, the boys getting a hoot out of this and making the racket to prove it.

Sam rolled, spitting dirt and dry pine needles out of his mouth, blood streaming from his nose. The acne-faced kid leaned down over Sam and scooped his arms under his legs. The bearded man squatted and took hold of Sam's chest, his whiskers smelling of cat piss, tobacco, and hooch.

They were near a riverbed where a dirt road led through red cedars and rosebud undergrowth, following the hills out of view. Beside them were weathered trestles. The skunky odor of sumac crept from the edge of the dark water, and above, spanning over the abyss, was an old black cantilever rail bridge that looked as if it hadn't been touched in over two hundred years. It seemed to sway, though Sam had a feeling it was him.

"We thought we'd give you a little tour of Versailles," the bald man said, pronouncing the name of the local town as if it could rhyme with kills. "First stop, the Kentucky River." He then fetched a knife out from the crotch of his pants, making a show of the gesture, mocking disbelief with his sloe-colored eyes. He cut the zip tie. Sam's wrists felt relief, but his arms had been bounded by rope knotted around his back and he still couldn't move. The bearded man secured a second rope around Sam's chest and arms with a trawling gyve at the back, its u-shaped shackle slightly bent. The man put a pin into place and locked the gyve.

Their going to hang me, Sam realized. There would be some sort of suspension at least. The ropes on him would hold, he hoped, but in the process they might tear the skin from his arms and chest and back.

The acned boy had disappeared from view.

"Hey, is the cable set?" the bald man called out. These did not seem the type of men to have a dependable plan. Yet they had some-how come before and set this all up, and now Sam saw the cable slung from the center of the bridge, its two ends meeting at an A-frame sup-port on the bank. On one end: the cable formed a loop with a ferrule. On the other end was a hook, which Sam could only imagine would go through the gyve on his back. He studied the diagonal line that the doubled-over cable made from the center of the bridge. He would hang eighty, maybe one hundred, feet over the water.

"Are we set up or what?" the bald man called.

"Ready to go," said the boy, who was sweating and grinning. The boy then went to the truck. He grappled a winch's hook loose from the vehicle's front bumper and worked the line out, lumbering toward the trestle, slipping the hook through the looped end of the cable hanging from the bridge. The other end of the cable was now free to hook onto Sam. The kid got a crazy look on his face.

"Don't fuck this up," the bearded man called out.

The boy winked at Sam, then slipped the hook through the gyve on his back and jog-trotted to the truck, where he locked the winch, then climbed in the cab and started gunning the motor. Sam understood. The taillights lit. The boy started to reverse and Sam began to lift from heels onto tiptoes and then off his feet altogether.

"Sayonara, cocksucker," the bald man hissed. "Or should I say bon voyage? If this don't kill you, you best get the hell out of Kentucky."

A string of violent unspeakables wailed through Sam's mind, but out of some stubborn pride or terror he remained straight-faced and silent as he was hauled up one hundred feet over the center of the Kentucky River, its dark waters equally silent and disturbing below.

From this new view, Sam could see the foreboding backside of the Wild Turkey distillery, and a billboard facing the road that read, "Bourbon lovers, welcome to heaven."

The big dipper came out, and Sam was getting cold. He had finally managed to wiggle one hand sort of free and got it into his pants. Out came the phone. He held the number two button down and it auto-dialed David. It went straight to voicemail. *If he's in that girl's bed...*

Sam had to hold the phone at his waist, which forced him to shout. "David! If you can hear me, I'm on a bridge at Wild Turkey. I'm stuck. I'm hanging here." The phone beeped, signaling the battery was low. Samuel breathed hard. "Come get me. Call the cops, call the feds." He hung up and quickly tried to dial 911. The phone died. A sharp pang shot from his chest into his neck. Sam breathed out, long and slow, trying to keep his head. *What now?*

He wriggled the hand with the phone back into his pocket and felt around for the knife deeper in, the rope burning into Sam's arm as he reached. *There!* The wood handle slid into his palm. Sam slowly pulled it out.

Press on dark spot in thuya burl... He tried to remember Renoux's instructions.

He held up the knife as far as he could and looked down, but couldn't see shit. He tilted the knife precariously, trying to catch some glint of the moon, his neck wracked with pain, and Sam squinted until he located a vague difference of color.

*while pulling left side of frame back and gripping with index finger at choil...*He only had one hand free. *If the knife slips?* He refused to think about it, pressed the left side of the knife against his waist, put pressure on the dark spot and slid the left side back.

Nothing.

"Come on, baby." This had to work; he would make this work. Sam's guts were churning. "Come on," he pleaded, the sound of his voice foreign and lost as it was swallowed by the indifferent night, and the water silent, too silent, far below. A breeze swept up, swaying Sam back a little. He heard something metal whine above him on the bridge and bumps rose on the skin of his arms.

"*Putain.*" This was absurd; Sam was alone, so alone. Where the hell was he? The adrenaline his glands had pumped over the last hours was making his body shake. He was simultaneously hot and freezing cold. He breathed out again, long through the nostrils, forcing everything out until his heart felt as if it would burst. Then he inhaled. Calmer, clearer.

Sam squinted down at the knife again. He couldn't feel his hand. There, another dark spot. He pressed his thumb down and repeated his actions, the knife hard against his belly as he pulled it back. This time, it released.

The blade sprung out, and Sam ran a finger along its edge—it was dull. He transferred his grip onto this false blade and held it as loosely as he'd dare, skimming the backside of his middle finger against the underside of the original thuya burl handle to check that a second, real blade was there. He then swung the knife out, butterfly-style, the thuya handle hitting the back of his hand and the hidden blade releasing out, then he rotated the handles and completed the motion, flipping the thuya handle down, and locking the blade into place.

A wave of energy rose up Samuel's spine. The pain from the ropes momentarily disappeared. Bending his wrist as far as he could, Sam worked the knife under the rope on his forearm and cut. The rope gave, and the blood rushed back into his hand. He then cut the rope from his other arm, and before he could register what was happening, his body slipped. He had failed to realize the rope around his chest had been looped under the ropes around his wrists, and without that perpendicular ballast, there was nothing to keep the rope from slipping up over his head. Sam fell, the water rushing up to meet him.

CHAPTER TWENTY FIVE

On the other side of the blackness was the light through David's eyelids. David had seen something deep under the earth—then felt a long stillness, like deep water. He groaned without opening his eyes. He could not remember what was under the earth, nor could he remember where he was, or how he had arrived. He saw orange, pink, and whiteness through the lids of his closed eyes. And he was wet.

He lay splayed on his back, the wind breathing on his arms and across the tops of his toes. He listened. The land smelled clean, rain raked, fresh, and he perceived all things without grogginess. His head throbbed, and his body seemed to know what his brain had lost—David's body told him to stay at rest. Stay down. Injured thing. Someone had done something, words were coming devoid of meaning, like the language of children. Last night, *quoi?* He heard Sam's voice, *quoi?* Then that was gone. I remember cats, William, and the porch and yard. Then what? Did you drink too much at dinner? Did I drink? What dinner? The word dinner felt too absurd. He had no desire to eat ever again.

He was thirsty. He was not sure if or how he could move. He felt more likely to fly. A wood-throated call of a bird, a dove, cooed, and David raised one eyebrow, bringing a wave of great pain that emanated from the back of his head and into his throat, through an eye and out of his forehead. The line of pain, strange in path, divulged nothing of its origins.

Is my spine broken? Can I move? He wiggled a big toe. He wiggled the other. Two things were clear: he was not in the Old Talbott Inn or wrapped in Clara's homespun sheets.

David decided, against better judgment, to look. He pried open a lid and could see the pillowy flesh around his eyes. Puddles near him reflected the thoughtless blue from the sky, and he saw the clawed feet of roots in rowed hillocks, hump upon hump, from which grew, of course—stalks of corn! *Tell me, young man, how did grass turn into corn?*

Ready to harvest, the corn was tan, paper dry, like huge grasses, sedge become stalk, perhaps—mutants, rustling like paper. He saw the black tips of the ears sway. David sat up, stretched his arms, got to his knees in the wet clay earth, and checked his pockets. He didn't have his phone. He had his wallet, but it had mud in it. He had the keys to the Firebird, but his shoes were nowhere to be found. *Where have I come from?*

The sun was overhead. *One o'clock? Two?*

There is a drifting way to all lost men—it unnerves the person, lost in a field, who knows this. This field was row after row, and David could not see above the stalks, but when he stood and jumped, he saw there was no edge in sight. Without sight trained on a landmark, a man would drift in his own direction. He needed to get a hold of Sam, and Clara, to figure out what had happened. He was suddenly anxious to get back to people.

There was no sense to it. Lost migrations of men and women, cut off from one another, would slope to their own broken compasses. Knowing nothing. Not Coriolis effect. No correlations. No clarity. Where were Clara and Sam? Where was he? As a chemist, he hated the senseless truths—the simplest questions no one could answer—*perhaps only a distant mathematician could? Peering down from the overhead blue, like sun.* David was delirious.

And yet, he felt weirdly fresh. He had learned something, but what?

Crows squawked, birds cooed. David did not know where the road was, but he started to walk through the stalks and leaves in the breeze, breaking each corn plant, then every other as he went to keep from veering and circling. But his own arc could be slight, David knew, unperceivable if he wasn't paying attention—and even with attention, he looked back and saw the line of half-bent stalks only so far.

He kept moving and bending stalks, his feet strong on the dirt and his breathing deep. He felt good. He walked a long while, then longer, the bending of stalks slowing his progress. His hands began to hurt. His head was still swollen, as was his neck. David looked back. He could see nothing but corn. Only bent stalks part of the way, then swallowed up in the field of tan, the movement of crinkled leaves in the breeze.

The road appeared, and David did not see it until, suddenly, it was there. Long two lanes, the double yellow, the pattern of macadam in the sun. He was blinded by thirst. It was now five o'clock perhaps. Four? He picked a direction and walked along the road, hoping he was heading toward town. Then, like a miracle, he saw the Firebird in a ditch. Parked.

CHAPTER TWENTY SIX

David climbed into the Firebird and flapped down the visor. A sunburned face looked back from the mirror, and it looked pretty bad. His crimson features were fixed high above a wide pale strip of neck where his face had cast a shadow during sleep—a sleep in which he had sensed something deep under the earth, but that was now lost to him, and he sat in the Firebird as if still in dream.

He was awake, though, the sting of the sunburn accounted for that. David appeared to himself like a pretend Indian, but he was not pretending. He was a man who had awoken in a field, drenched, without recollection, without reason. Had he done something? *What could I have done?* Also, what truth had faded while he strayed through row after row of corn, bending the stalks?

David flipped the mirror back up.

A thin cloud passed before the sun, and David recalled seeing a line of clothes set to dry somewhere. *Where?* He couldn't place it and recalled nothing more. He looked out into the day and upon the lone earth. Perhaps clarity would come with night? *Clara? Everything reminded him of her, but what was he not remembering?*

David looked in the tiny back seat, and saw his shoes and cell phone tossed haphazardly on the floor next to a newspaper and a bottle of water. *Why in hell would I leave them there?* He stretched around to grab his stuff, then pushed his seat all the way back to give him room to slip on the shoes. He left the laces untied. He'd been trying to guess the time as he wandered through the corn. Now in the bucket seat of the Firebird, he scanned the interior panels, the long display of the dash—each round gauge set across the board—but none were a clock. He turned the phone on and waited for it to boot up.

Take away a man's phone and put him beyond a visible road, make him forget where he has come from, and what does that man know? It used to be mankind was always waking up unsure of where he was, where he'd come from, and finding himself in some field, headland, heath, dell, lea, or ravine.

It was 4:43 p.m. David checked the missed calls, one from Sam, one from Lydia Dugranval, and several this morning from a Kentucky number he did not know.

He rolled down the windows, and started up the 'Bird, taking the road slow and easy back to Bardstown. He'd scarcely gone two miles, when the phone began to shake all over the passenger seat. He answered on speaker.

"Dubehash here."

"Where have you been?"

"Sam! I don't know what happened last night. I—What number is this?"

"It doesn't matter, David. You left me hanging, but I survived. I'm fine. Just a little sore," Sam said.

"What? Sam, I'm sorry...I don't remember."

"Listen, I need you to do something for me." Sam was terse.

"Samuel, do you have any idea what I did last night?" David croaked.

"I don't want to know. I need you to get over to Four Roses right away. You have to get into their rickhouses to search for barrels cut in the Japanese fashion, cut along the grain of the wood. I need you to get in there today. Find those barrels, and take samples from each."

"Sam, I need to figure out what—I mean, I found myself in a field today," David was fumbling, baffled.

"Get over to Four Roses, David, I need those samples tonight." Sam sounded angry. He wasn't listening.

"Sam..."

"Enough. I'll call you later. Meet me at Heaven Hill after you find those barrels. I lost my phone, so call me on this one. It's Parker's. I'll be sure to keep it on. And charged."

David listened to the message from Sam on the drive over to Four Roses, but it sounded garbled and windy. Something about Wild Turkey. Something about the Feds. Had there been a meeting between the Feds and Samuel last night at Wild Turkey? *Why there?* Did this have anything to do with his own condition?

He listened to the next message; it was Lydia asking him if he knew where Sam was.

Alert yet confused, David drove past the old abandoned office of Four Roses—its whitewash lit by the low sun to an almost crimson hue. The original distillery reminded him of an old jailhouse from the West, and passing it, David felt like he belonged in there—like he was the criminal, yet he was a good man he reminded himself. David also reminded himself that he and Samuel were on the side of justice, but who believed it? Not David. Something felt wrong—he had to get past the chemists at Four Roses and get inside the rickhouses by convincing them that he, David Dubehash, fellow chemist, was going to help them. *But how?* There would be tight security over the millions of dollars in booze held within, and who even knew what kind of extra precautions were being taken in response to the murder, including the presence of the FBI.

David shifted into second and drove over the bridge toward the distillery. He passed a swale of recycling waters, cooling and bubbling through green fountainheads just over the surface of the ponds. He smelled the slop from beyond the pond and saw the steam from the giant stills in the distillery. He had the nagging feeling that he'd done something to harm Clara. *Oh shit, Clara!*

He dialed her number but her phone was off. *All these stupid phones!*

David shifted, turned left, and roared in first gear up past the pillars, following the drive to the gift-shop parking lot and reception center where he parked the Firebird. "Clara, it's David. Call me please!"

The flags of Kentucky and the United States flew over the building. It would be getting dark soon, and he'd barely had a day, aside from waking in the bivouac of the field and finding his way out. David felt distant from the world of commerce and distilleries, an outsider to the state and country, even, which those limp flags represented. The lot was empty. The show was over, the only evidence of the cops and reporters was a Styrofoam coffee cup rolling in the breeze. David felt protective over Samuel suddenly. He also felt he had let him down, but he didn't know how. Whatever he'd done, he was determined to make up for it. He would get into those rickhouses, whatever it took.

David grabbed the bottle of water from the back and his sweater from the passenger seat. He stepped from the Firebird and splashed a little water onto his hands and worked the wet palm over his face and through his hair. He then patted himself dry with his sweater, put it on, and leaned down to tie his shoes. He locked the Bird and strolled casually, head up, working his shirt cuffs down from under the sweater arms as he approached the distillery.

Sam, meanwhile, was in Heaven Hill's fermentation room, studying each tank, sticking a finger into a vat and putting that finger, stippled in grain and foam, into his mouth. The mash had a sour, yeasty taste, the mixture of corn, rye, and malted barley, almost nutty beneath the astringent tang on the tongue. Sam had come here with the task of retrieving samples from the tanks to deliver to an old friend—pastry chef Francois Payard.

A rooster of a man in possession of a booming NYC bakery, Payard had a well-earned reputation as a genius chocolatier, not to mention the macaroons, the croissants, the fruit tarts…He was a man with the strut of genius in his walk and several secret recipes under lock and key. Payard's latest experiment was the creation of a bourbon truffle—a dollop of liquor inside a dark chocolate shell over a biscuit made from fresh sour mash. And despite the deep bruise around Sam's walloped eye and the searing pain in his left shoulder, the rope burns up his arms, the sharp pang in his ribs with every breath, the adrenaline hang-over in his spine, and the weight of mourning, fear, and loneliness in his core, tasting this mash made Sam feel good. At least there was hope in it. At least he was in collaboration with a creative mind out there that was as dedicated as he to coaxing the raw materials of this crude world into something palatable.

David entered the distillery offices at Four Roses, which were similar to the ones at William's GMO plant, but with an entirely different connotation. These were whiskey men. There were manuals on the built-in desks he passed, written in kanji, and containing English translations. A chemist behind a glass wall spotted David, looked at him strangely, then exited his lab to stand before Dubehash.

"Are you lost? The tour is closed for the day."

David saw no security, even though Woodrow had been murdered only days ago. *There must be cameras.* David gave the chemist a tilt of his head and slightly raised one corner of his mouth, then stuck out his hand directly, confidently, and said, "I'm David Dubehash, chemist and aspiring master distiller."

"And what can I do for you?"

"Well, uh, sir, I'm a student at the Institute of Fermentation, Maturation, and Distillation under Samuel Dugranval," David lied. "I'm working on my doctorial thesis, and my area of study is bourbon maturation."

"Oh, yes, Samuel Dugranval. He is in town, I heard." The chemist licked one of his front teeth under the security of his front lip, then smiled. "Pleasure to meet you."

"Yes, Samuel *is* in town. We had lunch today. In fact, he's staying at the Old Talbot Inn," David played up the naïveté, purposefully saying too much. "Samuel, in fact, is the one who said I should stop by now and talk to a master chemist about my thesis project—someone who reports to Jim Rutledge directly." David waited for the man to nod his head. "See I'm particularly interested in the temperature differentials, humidity levels, and airflow during maturation, resulting from the floor layouts of the rickhouses."

David saw a change in the eyes of the strange round man with the little face and his lies dispersed, slightly, and faded. The two men stood now in the presence of the language of science, of the applicable laws of absolutes, of Teleology perhaps—temperature, time, wood, char. The two thought together, nearly, as David explained a plan to monitor and map barrels and their locations within rickhouses, conducting a taste and chemical analysis on barrel samples over the course of a year and a half.

"This will be my doctorial thesis," David said, feigning boyish excitement, "and I think it will provide thought-provoking data." He jerked his head back slightly as if braking the Firebird. "Ideally I would like to do some of my research over at your Cox Creek rickhouses, as your rickhouses are single-storied, unlike most, as you know. Oh," David said, as if remembering something truly exciting, "and I have the opportunity, once I finish my thesis, to teach at IFDM. One of my courses will be on this very study, and I hope to keep monitoring your houses and reporting my data and findings back to Four Roses. I will send students to do this work after I have completed my initial study and thesis, and this can be an opportunity for you at Four Roses and us at IFDM to gather warehouse data over a long period of time," he said, wrapping up the pitch. "Samuel Dugranval will vouch for me." David smiled demurely. "Here's his card." David pulled a card from his mud-dried wallet, and took a pen and wrote his own full name and cell phone number on the back, then handed it to the chemist.

The chemist seemed flustered, then a wave of calm broke as he took the card from David and studied the finely embossed crest of IFDM on the heavy card stock. "Yes, I think this will be fine. Actually you might provide us with some useful information about our facilities. And who knows…" he agreed, not finishing this thought. "Step into my office, and I'll get you a security pass."

On the long drive to Cox Creek, David did not play music. He drove calmly. He got to thinking. Clarity came with night. He was driving through dry corn and horse estates, passing fences, birds on fences, and a small heard of deer nibbling on someone's crops.

David felt calm and contemplative. He thought of the owl he had seen in his mind swooping over Clara's home while talking to the chemist. He had a note on the Four Roses letterhead along with a security badge beside him on the passenger's seat. He remembered that home of Clara's. He thought of how much he liked it there—everything in its place. How he liked Clara—everything about *her* in its place, and he wanted to see her again. He wanted to get everything inside *him* into place. He questioned himself down to his true quiet self, and he guessed he'd been hasty about his feelings for Clara, but he also guessed he felt something promontory in her rising from the sea of women he'd known, and he guessed he wasn't going to give up easy—that it would probably be heartbreak for him, all of it.

He tried to call her again, but her phone was still off.

David stopped at a store and bought a pack of cigarettes with an Indian on the front. He smoked a cigarette on a hill outside of the Firebird and drank a root beer as he watched the last of the day die. The fields were dark gold in the red light, and the horses on a nearby farm whinnied and swished their ruddy hair on their necks. David couldn't stop thinking about Clara. He thought her name in his head so many times, but it was always as a question.

He forced himself to do guesswork over how he landed on his back in that field, just to change his train of thought. He thought about dosages of medication, the possibility of some sort of reaction or poisoning from the Cetirizine he took. He thought of the FBI. He thought of the local boys and perhaps a fight, maybe while drunk, but the pain in his head didn't match up. He considered alien abductions. He thought of Sam and some elaborate joke, but this was no time for joking. He thought of love and wondered if he would always be a man on the road alone, forever a sidekick to Sam.

David trudged back to the car, powered up the radio, and drove on. It was country, the same station as before. It grew dark. A last lightning bug of fall flickered, the first of the night. More appeared. The windows went down. He heard "Rambling Man" by Waylon Jennings, he heard "Ride Me Down Easy" by Willie Nelson, then he heard "A Place to Fall Apart" by Merle Haggard, and he arrived at Cox Creek, determined to get the samples for Sam.

There was a pond. David's shoes crunched gravel. Deer eyes, ears, and the shape of a head appeared, and a possum, blind, froze white and ratlike in his path. He saw the deer kick off and bound. He walked toward the first rickhouse, used his badge, and entered. Grazing in the distance was a herd of cows chewing the grass over the acres of rickhouses. *Lawn mowers*, he thought.

Cox Creek was made of acres of rickhouses, and this first house held barrels upon barrels upon barrels, stacked six high in numbered rows. *Cocksucker*, David thought, *It'll take years to look at them all.* If there were a thousand, that was only the start. David walked to a corner and dropped his sweater to mark the place where he started, then went down the row, looking up and down at each barrel. The lights overhead stung his eyes, and he could not clearly see the barrels up top.

There were rails, like train tracks, that went between the rows of barrels where a forklift could drive on its train-like wheels. David climbed up the stalls to see the top barrels and made his way down and up again along one line. His back already hurt, and looking up, down, and climbing only made it hurt worse. He tried not to think of the nineteen other warehouses waiting for him and made his way through ten rows of barrels. All American chopped staves were all he saw—cut any which way to get the most out of the oak.

The barrels were horizontally at rest, bungs up, and David continued to crawl up and down the stalls, scuffing his shoes, legs, and arms. His neck and back throbbed. He started to hunch a bit as he neared closer to the end of the first warehouse. There were so many. First he'd been in the endless corn, now in endless corn liquor. He gave up. He sat down on the floor. He got up. Started again.

He got through one rickhouse.

He got through two rickhouses.

He got through three.

By the fourth, he was holding his lower back and walking like an old man. If he didn't find them here, he wasn't going to anywhere. He couldn't climb anymore. He had to go by eye from below. The lights stung. He was hardly seeing, but he was seeing all right. He was seeing barrels.

Give up? No, he couldn't disappoint Sam.

In the sixth house, he got a gut feeling that nothing was there and left. In seven, he worked slower than ever and found a row of barrels tucked in a far corner, cut the Japanese way, and he nearly cried with relief.

David rested a moment, feeling slightly dizzy, and then nabbed a whiskey thief that was leaning near the door. The instrument was basically a giant hollow railroad spike, but the top housed a hole for the whole thumb to cover once submerged into a barrel through the bung. The pressure of the thumb sealed the liquid inside, like a great bartender's trick with a metal straw.

David got a thief's worth out of the first barrel, but had nowhere to put it, so he dropped it back in and limped out to the car to got the root beer bottles. He had bought a six-pack on the drive, but had only finished one. He emptied thee out in the grass.

Back inside the rickhouse, he used the thief and filled all the bottles, but there was still more whiskey to collect. He went back to the car, found a plastic bag in the trunk, doubled it by twisting it in the center to make two separate compartment, went back to the rickhouse, panting now, filled it with whiskey and tied it up.

CHAPTER TWENTY SEVEN

The late evening was Indian-summer warm, and Parker and Sam were sitting in the grass out back of a Heaven Hill rickhouse—the newly built one, erected for two million dollars on the same site where the old one had burned down. A lantern was set between the men. The distillery dog, Lucky, was curled up at Parker's side, and a make-shift table made from a barrel top was before them, upon which sat twenty-eight small glasses of bourbon, labeled and numbered. The two men sipped silently, alternating between taking notes, closing their eyes, and spitting in the grass. Several years back, Sam and Parker had set up an experiment in which they had taken a single batch of white dog and placed it into barrels at the cardinal corners of a rickhouse, on each floor, seven floors in all, with the goal of discerning the effects of barrel location on the maturation of whiskey. The differences were subtle but marked, and the two men kept their musings to themselves so as not to influence one another, and perhaps also because silence felt more comfortable conversation that night than any other to be had.

They had been sitting and tasting for the good part of an hour when Lucky suddenly perked up. The crunching of feet was heard, and Lucky let out a lighthearted yip to welcome Nathaniel Campbell, who was approaching. Parker and Sam turned and, squinting into the night, saw the silhouette of a man who looked half boyish, his jeans and button-up shirt worse for the wear. Tucked under Nathaniel's arm was a bulging cloth sack that clinked with his stride.

"A perfect night for a picnic, eh?" he said, looking out into the field beyond the men.

"Perfect timing," said Sam. "We were just completing a sampling of a small batch maturation experiment Parker and I have been playing with."

Nathaniel scanned the setup on the barrel lid. "Well I hope your taste buds aren't fried because I've brought a little experiment of my own," he said, and he broke into a full grin. It was the first time Sam had seen the boy's teeth since he'd been in Kentucky, and they were straight white pillars—a classic American farm-boy spread.

Parker raised a curious eyebrow, "Is this—"

"You bet yer socks it is," Nate replied, his eyes flashing with the glow from the lantern. He stepped in closer to the men and withdrew two small bottles from his bag, then stopped short. "Jesus, Sam, did you get trampled by a horse?"

"Oh, it was nothing," Sam lied, a hand self-consciously rising to his face. He wanted to protect Nathaniel from something, but he wasn't sure what. "I, *euh*, ran into some drunken ruffians at the race after you left. It looks worse than it feels."

"Shit, Sam, and here I thought you knew how to fight." Nathaniel leaned down and gave him a hearty slap on the shoulder.

Samuel winced but covered his reaction with a quick tit-for-tat. "Well if you hadn't gotten me so drunk, someone might have really gotten hurt." Sam even managed a convincing wink with his good eye.

"All right, Nathaniel," Parker chimed in, "it's about time we took this picnic up a notch. How about you give us a pour?" He perfunctorily dumped the contents of a glass in front of him onto the grass, and then poured water into the glass to rinse it out.

Nathaniel crouched, revealing sockless ankles, uncapped one of the bottles, and leaned in. "Now I want your honest opinions here. There's no need to tiptoe with me."

Lucky started to growl. Everyone turned. Staggering over a low bank of earth at their backs arose the form of a hunched and broken man.

"Who's there?" Parker called out, his voice suddenly brusque.

"Only a genius of deceit…"

"David," Sam said, but didn't say anything more; instead he stood up and watched wide-eyed as his assistant limped forward, bent and slowed, one hand spread across his lower back, the other hooked into the loop of a plastic convenience store bag.

"You know, every warehouse at Four Roses has a footprint of one acre, and I just walked through seven of them," David said. "Thank God it wasn't all twenty, or I might've had to put myself in traction." He then shuffled into the light, the lantern upcasting onto an exhausted face that sagged in the upper cheeks below the eyes, bloodshot and glazed. His nose and forehead were smattered with sun-blisters that looked ready to pop.

Sam looked at David angrily, but the kid looked so wilted he couldn't hold a hard gaze.

David looked back at Sam with eyes suddenly cleared by compassion and shock.

Parker Beam started laughing, really laughing, deep-bellied shakers at the sight of these two men who, within days of arriving in Kentucky, had been so physically transformed. Sam, once smart-shoed and dapper with not a hair out of place, now looked like some thoroughly roughened briar patch kid—his shoes a discolored mess, his face that of a rapscallion, scuffed, bruised, and torn. And David? Well the sweet Ohio cherub looked almost cynical now and ten years older, at least.

"That woman really took it out of you!" Sam finally said, his mouth forming a little "o" as he shook his head, and his eyes began to dance to the tune of Parker's laugh.

"Well I don't know if something was taken out of me, or something got into me, or if I even saw Clara last night for that matter, but Sam, what in the world—why didn't you tell me? I mean, who did this to you? I'm gonna break their necks!" David laughed nervously, affably, urgently.

"Well I did call," Sam said. The two friends locked eyes, and the past became the past.

Nathaniel, still crouched at the barrel top, looked up. "Well if there's one thing that could possibly heal your fellas' wounds, it might just be this," he said and poured a drink from one of the bottles into Parker's glass. He picked up three other tasting glasses, deftly fingering them with one hand, dumped their contents, and rinsed them out one by one. With more than a bit of trepidation, he then asked, "What were you doin' in the Four Roses' rickhouses, David?"

The mood barometer dropped.

"Well, uh—" David began to answer, but Sam broke in.

"Let's just say I had a little hunch and sent David over there. Let's taste first, Nate, then I'll explain." Sam looked at David questioningly. David nodded his head in confirmation and patted the plastic sack.

Nathaniel's shoulders fell in a momentary defeat, but then he raised a glass. "To my father," he said.

"To Woody," Parker said. And their glasses clinked.

It was the first time Sam had ever wanted to spit out something that tasted so good. It wasn't the whiskey. It was divine—a toffee sweetness stretching along the palate, simultaneously complex and clean, the definitive musk of Japanese oak, and a plum finish again, but there were also hints of sultana and cherry, and a robustness that lingered. He counted the caudalies, and noted how it changed on his tongue, coming out nearly peppery at the end, yet also sweet and thick. No, what made Sam gag as he sipped Nathaniel's product was that it was not what he had tasted at town hall with the FBI. This was something else completely. It was the same idea, of course, but a creation that elevated the concept to an utterly different level. This was not only a melding of American and Japanese technique and flavors; it was a third and entirely new thing greater than the sum of its parts. And moreover, it rang with a precision that screamed of the legends of Suntory and the legendary man, Woodrow Campbell. Sam was aghast.

Nathaniel watched Sam's response with confused horror. Sam looked like he was going to be sick, his features were fumbling in odd maneuvers. Parker, meanwhile, was utterly beside himself with delight. "Nathaniel, this is genius…"

"Four Roses is up to something," Sam blurted out. "I don't understand. Does this mean Kirin was the target and Four Roses was the victim, not Woody at all?" He then realized everyone was staring at him, and that everyone was lost. "Nathaniel," he said, "there's something I haven't told you. The night before last, the FBI called me in to taste some samples they found at the murder scene. Well, here, why don't you taste them for yourself?" Samuel looked at David, and David pulled out the root beer bottles from the plastic bag. He chose one of the darker samples and poured it into a glass for Nate.

Skeptical but trusting, Nathaniel took a sip. It took a moment, but then his face went white. "But, but…those fuckers stole our idea!"

Parker reached over and grabbed the glass out of his hand and had a sip for himself. He washed it around in his mouth, gave it a "Kentucky chew." For some reason, Parker seemed unsurprised. "Kirin's little experiment here is good, but it is decidedly inferior to yours," he said matter-of-factly.

Meanwhile David had been sipping silently, alternating between a coke bottle and his glass of Nathaniel's product. "What are the chances that a Kirin-owned distillery would be coming up with the same idea for a blending of Kentucky and Japanese traditions at the same time as a Suntory-backed consultant like your dad? I just don't get it." He paused, picked at something on his thumb, his expression no longer simply exhausted, his features showing the burden of a new kind of duress. "Was Kirin spying on you and Woodrow?" David popped his glance up from his hands and shot eyes at Nate. "Or was your father collaborating with Kirin behind your back?"

Nathaniel was serious, but not offended. "David, I know for a fact my father never gave any secrets to Kirin or even the lowliest person on the Four Roses staff. But I do know Suntory has been aware of our product for a while now, perhaps even longer than my father and I thought."

Calm, slow, and sweet Parker cleared his old throat a little, opened his mouth as if to speak, held back, looked around—everyone looked at him—then finally, out came the words. "Well I found out a few things today that may or may not offer some explanation to, uh…well, I heard some things, and I'll just tell them to you straight. I called up Jim Rutledge over at Four Roses this morning—you know he's an old friend of mine, and Woody knew him well too, though they were never particularly close, what on account of the tensions between their bosses and all. So I just right on and asked him what Woody was doing over at his fermentation house the other night. And, Nathaniel, you're right—your father was a loyal man." Parker paused and took a sip of Nathaniel's bourbon. "Rutledge told me that he had called Woody over because his head chemist had heard that Woody had been fired from Suntory, and he thought Woody might then be willin' to help him with a new product that Four Roses was going to try to release before the end of the year. They were havin' some troubles gettin' the mash bill right, something in the marriage was off. But apparently, Woody refused to help on account of he was trying to work things out with Suntory, said he needed to be extra careful of every step he took. Wouldn't even taste the stuff to offer an opinion, Rutledge told me, because Woody felt sure he could get his job back." Parker met eyes with each of them as he told this, and his voice lowered down to a near whisper. "He also told me something else, something that frankly no one else except his head chemist knows. Really I shouldn't be tellin' y'all, but well, considering the circumstances and all, and what with you sharin' this exquisite drink, Nate, I'll be damned if it ain't my duty to tell." He swallowed another sip hard. "See Rutledge told me there are rumors that Kirin is entertaining a merger with Suntory."

"What?" Nathaniel exclaimed.

"Think about it, Nate." Parker slung back as if he'd been thinking about it himself all day. "Suntory is huge, a goliath. They own Yamazaki and Hakushu in Japan, distilleries including Bowmore in Scotland, Louis Royer in Cognac. What else? They own Midori, Shochu, Château Lagrange in Bordeaux, Pepsi Nex in Japan, the list goes on and on. Hell, I think they're even in the ice cream market with Häagen-Dazs, and they own the most popular bottled mineral water in Japan. Of course, the rivalry between Kirin and Suntory goes way back, and the competition in this industry, as we all know, can get hot, but we're talkin' about big corporations here, and in big business, it all comes down to big wigs lining their pockets. This is about money, boys. Kirin ain't no small hops either, we know, what with Four Roses—and God bless them for their beer—but still, they're a smaller company and would benefit from Suntory's resources. I mean, just imagine if the companies merge. That's some global coverage to say the least." Parker leaned back and let his news sink in.

The men were quiet for a while, then Sam, wanting to ease the thick air, spoke. "In this day and age, Parker, family-owned distilleries like yours, like this glorious preserve here," he gestured toward the Heaven Hill rickhouses that surrounded them, white and glowing walls contrasting with the black torula creeping up their flanks, "it seems like they are becoming extinct." Sam looked into Parker's eyes and was suddenly thanking him. "You're a rare bird, Parker Beam, you really are."

Nathaniel was furrowing his brow, something bubbling within his guts. "So you think it was Suntory that gave our idea of a Japanese-style bourbon to Four Roses because they couldn't get it from my father and because they were going to own Four Roses pretty damn soon anyway?"

"That's exactly what I think," Parker replied. "Rutledge told me that the new product they're working on came from the head chemist, and he most likely got the idea from someone higher up. Rutledge didn't know you and your father were workin' on something of your own. He was just going to an expert for help."

Though this indeed was news to everyone, Sam couldn't help but feel that nothing had been explained. He couldn't stop thinking about the knife. Not Renoux's that was in the silt of the Kentucky River, forever lost; he couldn't stop thinking about that sushikiri knife in the fermentation tank. Who would have done such a thing? It seemed a crude attempt to frame the Japanese, but which Japanese? Kirin or Suntory? And why? To stop the merger and reinvigorate the long-standing antagonism between these two companies? And why Woody?

A warm wind came up as the men sat gazing into the dark, whiskey heating their bellies, conspiracies and rancid vengeances unsettling their minds. Parker Beam began to talk long and low about this land that had been in his family so long. He spoke about the big fire that had happened a little over a decade back. Seven of Heaven Hill's forty-four rickhouses had burned to the ground, with seventy-five mile-per-hour winds stoking the flames to nearly five times the heat of the Chernobyl accident. The ignited whiskey had seeped from the fallen rickhouse frames, pouring downhill and into the river, and the water that flowed through Bardstown burned.

"But we had good neighbors," Parker said. "Though they were our competitors, the good folk at Brown-Forman and Jim Beam stepped in after the fire and provided production to keep our business going. That's the kind of men we bourbon men are, and Lord help us come the day our neighbors turn us out."

That night, David couldn't sleep. He had moved out of the haunted room, taking refuge in the Pleiades suite next door. Sheets tangled between his legs, and he tried to remember another story of a fire he had heard. Something William had told him at the GMO research facility. Something about corn. He pushed his eyes far back into his head, searching for a detail that would unravel it all, but he only entered into syrupy darkness where a strange smell lingered. *A rotting plant?* Then nothing.

CHAPTER TWENTY EIGHT

"**T**hey weren't tourists, that's for certain, but the entire state of Kentucky is a small town. Everybody's somebody's family, and no one will talk." Downstairs at the lobby desk, David found Sam the next morning on the phone with his wife. "I know, dear, but really, there's not much more I can do." Sam was dressed in a blue suit, no tie, his hair neatly combed. His pallor was good, and the purple and black ring around one eye shone undeniably in the light.

David ambled to find a coffee mug, filled it, then took a seat in the dining room. Sam finished his call, and joined him.

"So…" David took a swill of coffee, "what happened to your face?"

Sam tried to blow the question off. "Just some drunks roughhousing at—"

"What, they sucker-punched you and stole your phone?" David wasn't buying it.

Sam shook his head, sighed, and told the whole story. He told David about being too drunk to defend himself, about being hit in the backs of the knees while pissing. He was bitter and hurried dully through the tale. When Sam came to the gray truck, David jumped in his seat.

"I told you about that truck, Sam! I told you we were being followed." Samuel shot him a dirty look. "Would you let me finish, David?"

David regained his composure, fidgeting with his American red and blue tie, his half Windsor knot, the cuffs of his shirt. They were about to have brunch with a local legend, the grandson of Old Julian "Pap" Van Winkle, Julian Van Winkle III, and both he and Samuel were dressed for the affair.

David felt like a culprit. It didn't help that Sam eyed him at each point when the story got worse, giving him a particularly callous look when he recounted calling David with the last of the battery on his cell phone. But David knew his innocence and became enrapt in Sam's story about being lifted up one hundred or so feet above the Kentucky River and the subsequent plunge into the water, which, thank God, was deep.

"The bastards! This wasn't just some prank."

"The local cops questioned everyone on the Churchill Downs maintenance staff last night, but everyone's playing stupid."

David's fists were unconsciously balled up. There was something crawling around in his head, but he couldn't put a finger on it. "I think I've been drugged," he said. "Yesterday, I mean." He tried to explain there was something about his thought process today, to the feel of the world—a distance between him and the objects of the inn, and between he and himself. How else could he explain waking in a cornfield with no memory? Plus the strange elation and oneness in the field yesterday and the leftover state he now felt? It wasn't booze that landed him in that field—not from drinking anyhow, he claimed. "Sam, I know I let you down not answering that call, but I believe I was knocked out and administered a drug."

Sam squinted his bad eye, winced slightly, and twisted his mouth, "Oh, here we go."

"Samuel, I'm serious. I have no memory of what happened to me two nights ago. Dropping you at the racetrack, I went to see William. I have no memory after William's GMO plant other than a fragment of my arrival at William's house. Late the next day, I wake up in a cornfield, with no shirt, the back of my head throbbing, and I have no memory." David's face was dire. Sam listened, as incredulous as the story was, and tried to imagine those local buffoons drugging David—baldy, the man with the beard, and the pink-faced boy. It was unlikely. They weren't stealthy enough, nor did they seem the sort of men to know how to administer drugs to anything but a roped calf, perhaps, or a mule.

"Didn't you tell me, David, that you and William once indulged in entheogenic substances?" Samuel shot David a stern look. "Are you sure you didn't take something with him again? Peyote or something?"

David scowled, then thought of the possibility that William had slipped him something. *No.* That wasn't likely. William was older now, as was David, and a decade had passed since they were college boys. William wouldn't slip David anything, would he?

"Come on, we're going to be late." Samuel nodded, sipped from a glass of water, chomped a few ice cubes, and stood. "I don't know *what* happened to you, but I won't hold it against you—let's just be very careful. By the way, you did a fine job getting into those rickhouses last night, and you really came through, David. Or should I call you...what did you call yourself? A genius of deception?"

Sam wasn't getting it. He tried to make a joke of what David was saying, tried to lighten the mood, but it wasn't to be made light of. David's mind was clouded over, and he stood up and finished the coffee in one fast slurp. He saw his hand move down to his side and slip the mug onto the table; he was amazed at his acuity. There *was* something funny going on, and it wasn't laughable. He had a sense, for a moment, of something—a premonition, and through the hard crust of the blackness of his hidden memory, something appeared like an angelic woman, then was gone. It was a moment of whiteness and clarity, in which he understood something being told to him, then it was over.

Outside Lexington, they found Julian Van Winkle III's estate. It was a horse farm, and as they drove up the gate, they saw Julian's award-winning sire, Fenceline, true to its name, trotting alongside the fence.. The home was sophisticated but downplayed, with lots of tan woods and stone. They parked behind a hedge of high shrubs and ambled across a great sea of smoothed stones toward a path running up to a wooden door right out of a fable, dome-shaped and heavy with large metal rings.

David knocked, and Sam cleared his throat. The door was opened down the middle, and one of the sides of the domed doorway swung open. Julian Van Winkle III stood before them with his bald head, deep set eyes, forward-jutting mouth, and white whiskery mustache. He looked old and humble, satisfied, sure of what he was, a third generation whiskey man who kept alive the legend and legacy of his grandfather, brewing and distilling twenty-year-old "Old Pap" bourbon. Among its cult following, "Old Pap" was believed to have no peer— and Sam and David both respected the brand.

"Sammy," Julian said, "and David, right?" His thick white mustache covered his entire upper lip.

"Thanks for having us, Julian." Sam shook Julian's outstretched hand, and the two embraced stiffly, like men who did not know each other well but had respect for each other. David stuck out his hand, and they, too, shook.

"Come in, come in. I made tons of food." The three men entered the small castle, a sea of reclaimed woods, long communal tables, bookshelves, fine rugs, and tapestries. A stone fireplace stood in the room off the kitchen, and a sliding glass door led out to a walled garden.

They sat at a community-style table between the kitchen and living area, upon which heaps of food steamed in the room. German sausages glistened alongside plates of scrambled eggs, pancakes with blueberries, and a bowl of hot spinach with pats of butter. It wasn't fancy. It was down-to-earth home cooking, and David's eyes grew wide with delight. Stone ground mustard was in a mortar. David was famished. He thought back to yesterday and realized he hadn't eaten anything since he awoke in that field.

David loaded up a plate of food, free from all manners, pulling the hot sausages onto his plate with his fingers. Julian and Sam laughed. "Looks like he's hungry," Julian said. "Hope you brought your appetite too, Sam." Sam gave a warm chuckle. "There's more food than we can eat," Julian said, and sat down, and so did Sam, dishing their plates as David dug in.

They mostly sat in silence and ate like men among men. There was not much to say, a little talk of the race here and there, and the necessary things said honoring Woody. Julian looked a few times at Sam's eye, but asked no questions, and Sam did not proffer explanations. David ate three plates of food as the two men watched him with a mix of admiration and disdain. David had some egg on his chin and a bit of syrup at one corner of his mouth. He wiped his face with a napkin.

What are we doing here? David didn't get this—how Sam worked. It was time to put the pieces together, to go after those guys with the gray-and-white flatbed truck who had abducted Sam. It was time to get to talking with the FBI—with Lefevre.

"So how have you two enjoyed Kentucky so far?" Julian asked, studying Sam and David. David finished the plate, his expression drenched in post-food sleepiness, and Sam, with the strange black eye contrasting with his fine style of dress, leaned back in a contented yet formal repose.

"So far, it's been great," Sam said, and bit into a sausage link he'd cut into thirds with his knife. "Right, David?" He chewed.

"Right."

Something kept getting at David. He knew there was revelation just below the surface. That angel he'd seen had not returned, but he sensed she was close. The moment of clarity had to come. It was humid outside today, and the day was stretching on into early afternoon. It wasn't so different from waking in that field yesterday, in terms of weather, except there was no breeze. Julian's home had central air, which cooled them, but the humidity still crept all around, making it hard for David to focus. He was so tired. His eyes burned. He felt dull, and Sam seemed far away in his own little world as well. It was time to move. Where was that angel of clarity?

"How about a drink and some cigars?" Julian offered just after Sam finished the last of his sausage.

"Good idea," David said, and Sam agreed. Tobacco was a good start, and a drink couldn't hurt. "Have any of that twenty-year Pappy Van Winkle Family Reserve?" David asked.

Julian laughed. "You've come to the right place." He brought out a bottle, and they all retired to the back patio with their tumblers and cigars—short 35-minute smokers, easy on the draw, not complex, which went fantastically with the complex long-lasting spirit. They sat in white iron chairs and passed a torch around.

"I've always said you cannot enjoy a cigar and a drink if one is in competition with the other," Sam said, and Julian nodded his head in respectful agreement.

The men smoked, and birds chirped in the humidity, even though it was late fall. Maybe rain would come. They sipped their bourbon, and Sam and David thanked Julian for the good food and the hospitality, saying nothing about why they were in Kentucky.

David studied Julian, and smoked his cigar. A strange feeling came over him. He stopped blinking. The angel was around, he sensed. He saw purplish webs and emulations coming from the sides of his vision, yellows as well. Julian began to take on connotations alien to himself, and David watched him chewing on the end of his cigar. He had seen something under the earth. Long ago, he had been under the ground in a hovel around a fire, and a woman had chewed corn and spit it into a pail. He had watched the old woman, her wrinkled face dark and leathered, wrinkles coming from her nose across her cheeks in long deep lines. He watched Julian chew and saw lung shapes in the yellow and purple visions, forms of old women and men, unborn children, orbs and ovulations, faces and long noses—the woman he had seen, she spit corn into a pail. She looked at him with uwavering eyes, flat and glossy with cream upon the pupils, and she chewed the corn and spit it into a pail held in her wide, calloused hands.

"Sula," she'd said to him. "Sula." It all came back to David.

He dropped his drink into the grass. "Sam, I wanted to see Clara after William's GMO plant!"

Sam turned.

"I went to William's house. I didn't drink anything, then I left. William's mother was angry with me. I broke into Clara's, and there was a still. She was moonshining, but no one was home. Or I thought so. Then I went into her basement and someone hit me from behind. I was hit on the back of the head, three times, and woke up in—"

"What? What are you saying, David?" Sam nearly choked on his drink.

Julian almost laughed, standing up as well. "Clara Stillwater? Oh, boy, watch out for those Stillwater girls. I knew Perley when she was

149

a young woman. Nearly shot my head off with a sixteen gauge one night." Julian chuckled to himself. David was still seated.

"David, if this is true, you need to call her." Sam's mind was spinning, and spinning fast. "Call her and tell her you need to see her tonight. Tell her we are leaving Kentucky for good tomorrow, that we have finished our corn investigation. Get her to meet you someplace, or pick her up, take her to dinner, just get her out of the house."

"Stillwater girls." Julian chuckled to himself. "You never know what lies beneath the surface."

David called Clara from the road.

"Why, Mr. Dubehash, I was just thinking about you."

David's heart was flying in his chest, warm and throbbing away to its strange rhythms. He felt light-headed, and he realized what he'd done. He'd told Sam he was attacked in her basement. He did it in front of Julian. He was destroying everything in one fell swoop—and for what? What did he care if she hit him in the back of the head?. She could knock him out all she liked. He remembered the sour smell and mildew mixed with the bready hooch-brewing scent in the basement. He remembered his coffee cup in the sink. He felt protective over her, even as he betrayed her.

"Clara, I'm leaving tomorrow and I need, I mean, I want to see you," Sam nodded, and David wanted to hit him in his good eye for that nodding. "We finished our research. We are going to New York tomorrow." David said it as if he had never been less excited about anything, "Let me pick you up and take you to dinner tonight? Oh, and Clara, sorry about two nights ago. I should have met up with you, but I think I got drunk with an old friend, and I woke up in a field. I feel like a fool." He felt like a liar.

"Sure, David. We could get something to eat," Clara said, hesitantly, then with too much willingness. "Pick me up at my place at, say, six o'clock?"

"Sure, that's good," David said. "See you then." He hung up.

"Breathe, David," Sam instructed. "Take a breath." Sam took David's phone and used it to call Lefevre. "Agent Lefevre? Sam Dugranval. I have a lead on something you'll want to look into, I believe. Someone who's brewing illegal hooch. Here's the chance for you to play cops and robbers with a real bootlegger. You interested? The operation will be left unwatched tonight. Want to go check it out with me?" Sam was selling. "Remember you owe me one after that night at town hall."

Lefevre agreed. They were to meet at the inn at six that evening, and Sam would bring him over. "David, you're doing the right thing. If it's just a still, I'll convince Lefevre to leave her alone. We will take a look and see what's over there. Hell, this whole thing could just be jealousy. Maybe a man got jealous and knocked you over the head. Maybe his friends are the ones with the truck. It might just be local boys protecting their women. Or it might be something else."

David didn't say anything. Why had he blurted out all that information? He was hating himself now. He'd been in a sort of trance. He got out his cigarettes in front of Sam.

"I knew you were smoking again." Sam grinned "You think I couldn't smell them on you?"

David lit up, shaking. David felt lower than anything he'd ever thought possible. He wished he knew nothing. He wished he were a whiskey man, not a whiskey dick.

CHAPTER TWENTY NINE

Clara's front door was unlocked. Sam wasn't sure how Lefevre had finagled a warrant so fast, or even if he had managed to acquire one at all, but no matter. That was his problem—Sam was just along for the ride. Whether in the lab, or on the street, or in the bedroom, for that matter, Sam approached the world with the mantra that no idea was too crazy, so long as you were prepared, meticulous, and did it right. In this case, doing it right meant getting someone else to do it—a professional.

Lefevre was all fired up, his eyes catching light like two shiny pistols. The agent had transformed into a bootleg buster, fancied himself a glorified noir hero, no doubt, rough and romantically unromantic, a man in a coat broad-shouldering his way into subterranean dens, hot on the scent of illicit hooch.

All the lights were off inside, the house quietly creaking at its seams. On the kitchen table, a pair of earrings flashed in the moonlight—two silver foxes with turquoise stones for eyes. There was a dry smell in the air, a mixed bag of herbaceous Kentucky dust.

"Basement," Lefevre whispered and crept into the living room. Sam followed suit, the dark forms of three women embroidered on a tapestry watching him from the opposing wall. Lefevre tried a door to their right, opened it, gave Sam a nod, and headed down. The plank stairs squeaked under the agent's weight, and Sam was close behind, stepping as quietly as possible given the age of the house. Given these stairs had endured the swelling and retraction of the seasons year after year—

"What was that?" Lefevre's head flipped around. Samuel stopped, held his breath, but didn't hear a thing, save his own heart and Lefevre's heavy breathing. Lord, this was all too much. *What a scene we're creating. Anyone else, anyone normal, would just wait for tomorrow and come knocking on the door in broad daylight.* They continued down.

In the basement, Sam could just make out the shelves of bottles David had described. They went to the trap door and found it bolted, but Lefevre didn't miss a beat. He texted the tech van outside to bring in some bolt cutters, then set about snooping around for signs of unsanctioned activity. Sam stayed where he was, unsure if Lefevre could smell it, but certainly *he* could—a grainy humidity mixed with the scent of wet animal hair: the smell of pure-corn bourbon being distilled. Sam squinted at the jars on the shelf, trying to make out their contents. *What had she used to drug David?* he wondered. If only he had some light, perhaps he could deduce the poison from the ingredients here. Sam selected a bottle with dark, bulbous pods inside, went to open it, perhaps identify the contents with his nose, but someone was coming down the stairs.

One of Lefevre's lackeys in dark suit pants and an ill-fitting T-shirt came with the bolt cutters, and with impressive speed and efficiency, made a broken plaything out of the lock. He then heaved up the trap, and Lefevre stepped down. Sam went feet first behind him and had just stepped into a dim light of what appeared to be a laundry room distillery—flour sacks and duffel bags, body odor and steam—when a small explosion was heard. Something white flashed across the room and struck Lefevre in the gut, sent him flying back into a brick wall where he crumpled to the floor.

A barrel of a man in long johns and no shirt came screaming at Sam, senseless, shrieking, primal in his presyllabic war cry. The sound took Sam back to the Muay Tai ring, triggering his fight or flight reflex. That mass of flesh kept coming at him, and Sam pivoted, using the force of hips and leg as well as the man's own inertia, delivering his spinning back kick to the neck and ear. The big man flew into the wall next to Lefevre, trying to stop his head with his hands, as he struck, then crumpled. Still conscious, the man rolled over, groaning, and cradled his skull in between his hands as if heard some awful sound.

Lefevre was coming to, and in a slightly disoriented state, he'd seen Sam deliver the spinning kick. He looked stunned, confused, utterly at a loss, and was silent for a good thirty seconds before slowly, he began to laugh, clutching his ribs. "Samuel Dugranval, never in my life!" Sam did not laugh—he reached out a hand to help Lefevre up.

The FBI lackey had come downstairs at the sound of the commotion and was now cuffing the shirtless man. Sam and Lefevre turned their attention to the shiny copper still. In a deep corner of the sub-basement, the oblong tank had been soldered to a smaller dimpled column with an ingenious solid leakproof seam construction. A cap arm reached out from the top of the still, and bent at ninety degrees, connecting into a tall worm box to which a water hose from the wall had been connected on the upper left side in order to continuously carry cold water in to cool the alcohol vapors in the worm. Another hose came out the opposite side and broke at a drain in the floor. A spout also jutted from the worm box about halfway up, and below it sat a filtered glass carboy jug.

Sam reached out and touched the side of the tank, nay, caressed the side of the tank, and felt the residual warmth from the batch that had been run earlier that day. "This family must take a lot of pride in their distilling," Sam said quietly, as if to himself. "This copper has been polished nearly every day, which is rare indeed. You know, I always look for a dull still when more reflux is needed." He turned to look at Lefevre.

Lefevre called for backup.

"There's something more to this story," Lefevre was saying as he picked up the potato gun—the weapon that had badly bruised his abdomen, perhaps broken one of his ribs. Lefevre approached the hulking man, who had stopped screaming, but was now sobbing like a little boy, refusing to speak. Lefevre stared him down for a moment, then reached around his back and scanned one of his fingertips with the camera in his iPhone. The phone beeped, sent out a signal, and after some delay, came back with the identity and criminal record of one Ely Stillwater.

"He's clean," Lefevre said. "Only thing we got on him is a bestiality charge six years back."

"And a trouble-making sister, or cousin, or whatever the relation is," Sam replied.

Sam heard steps overhead—the forensics team had arrived—and within minutes, the underground distillery had been taken over by those same white coveralls and masks he had seen at Four Roses mere days before. A small beady-eyed man with an unfortunate nose whispered something into Lefevre's ear, then with urgent assiduousness, the crew began dusting and photographing everything in sight. Sam hollered at them not to touch the still. That beautiful piece of equipment he knew would not fare well if it was dismantled. He tried to explain, but the beady-eyed man wasn't listening. He only looked to Lefevre, and when Lefevre nodded, he stepped away from the still indifferently and started to examine the laundry hanging nearby on a wire, where it could catch the heat of the tank. "These stains look like blood," he said, and proceeded to signal for a man with a camera to photograph the belly-warped T-shirt before cutting off a piece of the cloth and slipping it into a plastic bag.

"Listen, Sam, it looks like you've led us to something a little more serious than moonshine," said Lefevre. "A lot more serious actually. My boys just told me that this here Ely Stillwater works at Four Roses, and he's been missing since the night of the murder." Sam swung his head around to where the cuffed man had been sitting on the floor, but he was already gone, hauled off by one of the agents to be interrogated in the van or some dungeon-like room in town hall.

Sam thought about David, off with Clara on the town, and his guts churned. She had already hurt him once, who knows what she was capable of a second time around. He picked up his phone and pressed down number two.

"Yell-o," said David. He had one hand on the wheel, the other on Clara's leg. The phone was resting in his lap. "You're on speaker phone, Sam, my Kentucky belle is here by my side. Say hi, Clara."

Sam heard a giggle, and he panicked, hung up.

"Must've been a pocket-dial," David said, raising his eyebrows and scrunching his shoulders into a light-hearted shrug. It had been a fine date. Clara had gone all out, greeting David on her front porch in a vintage chiffon cocktail dress from an era long gone—black with a low beaded neck, and recently rehemmed to show plenty of leg. They had gone to Limestone Restaurant, a stuffy, chair-padded place where David had been the tallest man in the room by a foot, and Clara, well, quite simply, she turned everyone's heads. They had eaten heartily—five courses, chef's choice: salads of Kentucky limestone Bibb, shrimp 'n grits, veal broth burgoo, stuffed rainbow trout for her, barrel-smoked rib eye for him, and David had ordered a Clos Vougeot Grand Cru, Domaine Christian Confuron from 2005 that was way out of his price-range, then a second bottle just for the hell of it. Somewhere between the appetizers and entrees David forgot that he was setting Clara up, but by dessert he had remembered again, but still didn't care. *Let her moonshine all she wants. Let her drug me and drag me anywhere she pleases.* The wine had gone to his head.

However, driving top down, the wind swept away his buzz, and when they rounded the bend into the last stretch of Clara's driveway, a ring of police cars and the telltale forensics van came into view. David was surprised—*why had they brought the whole team?* He felt Clara's whole body stiffen beside him.

"What's going on?" She gasped, "Oh, God, Ely!"

David looked at her, a bit in shock himself, not knowing what to say, feeling horribly responsible. "Who's Ely?" he said, then he saw the bulking man, hunched over, in the back of one of the police cars.

"You, you bastard!" Clara turned to David, face flushed, eyes like teeth tearing at David's skin. She jumped out of the car running to Ely, pressing her hands on the glass.

"But he didn't know any better," she screamed at an agent.

Meanwhile inside, the forensics team was looking for a knife. "We're looking for something double-edged," Lefevre called out, remembering Sam's observations that night at town hall. "Something about a foot and a half long, about twelve inches of blade."

Inch by inch, they were turning over the entire basement. Two of the younger agents on the team walked along a back wall, scanning the bricks with a portable X-ray machine that sent a digital feed back out to the tech van.

"Boss, there's something behind here," one said. The men suddenly were pulling out loose bricks from a sealed-off doorway, other agents joining in, until a space was clear. Lefevre shoved his way between his men and stepped through.

Clara was in tears, a flapped over rag doll, one arm in the nasturtiums on the porch. She had told everything, how her brother had come back that night covered in blood, terrified and feverish, shaking with chills. How he wouldn't let her burn his clothes, and so she had scrubbed and scrubbed until her blood mixed with the blood of Woodrow Campbell. How she was the one who had gone back and put the sushikiri knife in the vat in order to frame Kirin's staff, and how she had been ranting on and on to her brother about the Japanese invading Kentucky. "When he heard Rutledge tell Woodrow about the merger, he thought that was what I would have wanted him to do." Clara gasped in urgent chunks of air, as if suffocating. "Can't you see how impressionable he is? I am the responsible one. Take me in his place."

"Flashlight," Lefevre said, and someone slapped one into his hand. He flipped it on, and the beam shone into a vast subterranean warehouse: barrels lined and stacked twelve by twelve by twelve. Lefevre's phone beeped. "We've got a confession," the text read.

CHAPTER THIRTY

Sam walked through the vast cache of moonshine, searching for the oldest-looking barrels. His heart palpitated with excitement and disbelief; he had hit the mother lode. He stopped at a discolored barrel in a musky corner, wiped some dust off the bunghole, and lifted the whiskey thief he had found in the other room. "How about we taste the hooch?" he said, eyes sparkling with elation and mischief. "We should taste this and toast to the solving of Woodrow's murder." Sam removed the bung and plunged the thief into place. One of the agents produced several mugs taken, presumably, from upstairs. Sam pushed his thumb to cover the hole, raised the thief and poured its contents into one mug and then another.

"I don't know," Lefevre attempted to appear doubtful, but it was clear he wanted to partake. "I'll drink to new friends," Lefevre said. "Is that too hokey?" he asked. He held the glass level with Sam's. "You know, I don't hate alcohol," Lefevre said. "I'm not a killjoy. My old man was a drunk," he said and winced, grimaced, tried to compose himself, then clinked glasses with Samuel Dugranval. "To new friends and peace for the deceased," he boomed. He and Sam drank.

"Well said, Lefevre. And I must say, I can't bear the abuse of alcohol." Sam embraced the FBI agent in an out-of-character bear hug, and Lefevre laughed. Sam released him. The two gave one another looks of esteem and finished their glasses.

There's something familiar about this hooch, thought Sam.

That night at the inn, Sam and David sat in the Lincoln Suite. They each held a drink of Clara's whiskey. A fire burned in the fireplace. Sam had his feet up, and David had his hands together. "Taste that?" Sam asked. "Taste that corn?"

David nodded.

"David, you have got to cheer up. What can I do?"

"Nothing," David said. He sipped the moonshine. "Yes, I taste it." he said. The fire lit the room, and Sam looked like a shadow of himself, feet up on the ottoman. "Sam, that girl is the one for me," he mourned. "She didn't do anything wrong." David became angry with himself, or her, or Sam—he didn't know.

"She didn't do anything wrong?" Sam said. "What on earth are you saying?"

"She covered up for a half-wit brother who was misguided. It's awful what happened to Woodrow, but it seems senseless all around now. She never deliberately hurt anyone, including me." David was passionate. Sam could see his eyes lit with something that no man could refuse. A moment of anger shot up in Sam, as these were Woody's murderers, but it subsided, and Sam was forced to admit to himself that David was making some sense.

"She's a proud, willful woman," David said. "I am still very much in love, and tomorrow I am going to talk to Perley."

"Tomorrow we go back to New York," Sam said, "so you better be up early and get over there." His mouth curved up at the corners. "Look, David, you did the right thing. It might not look like it now, but you did. You solved this mystery, and what you've done—if the corn in this bourbon matches Barclay's, as I think it will—for whiskey alone is a miracle. You know Mrs. B. called an hour or so ago with a carbon dating of Barclay's whiskey."

"And?"

"Well it's not two hundred years old…it's closer to five hundred!" Sam's face finally betrayed a pleased grin. "It's the oldest whiskey ever found in America. It dates back to just after Columbus." Sam laughed and poured himself another drink of aged moonshine.

"That's great, Sam," David said half-heartedly. "I think I'm going to turn in if you don't mind." David stood.

Sam stood. He placed a hand on David's shoulder. "You did terrific work, David. You don't see it, and maybe you never will, but you're a man I respect." David could not see why. His throat swelled a bit, and his eyes burned. He nodded and went out of the Lincoln Suite, found his way to the Pleiades Room, undressed, and looked at himself in the mirror. He laid down, but could not sleep.

David got up, dressed, found a hat he had packed, which had been in his family a long time—three or four generations back, an old bowler that looked like what he imagined a lawman or an outlaw would wear in Kentucky long ago. He dressed in jeans and a dark shirt. He took the Firebird and drove to town hall. He found Lefevre. It was early in the morning or late at night. He grabbed Lefevre by the arm when he found him, entering a knife into a bag—the knife presumed the true murder weapon found hidden in one of the barrels in the subterranean Stillwater store.

"I need to talk to you," David said, uneasily eying the knife. "Find us someplace to talk?" he looked him deeply in his eyes.

"What do you need, David?" Lefevre looked tired. He brought them into a room meant for interrogation, and David pled Clara's case. He knew she would not get off free, but he wanted kid gloves treatment for her and her brother.

"Listen, your girlfriend's not just some protective sister. She sent those rednecks after Sam. I don't know why, but she was trying to scare you two out of town."

David took a deep breath, a sting of pain stabbing across his chest. He shook his head.

Lefevre put a hand on his shoulder. "But this woman sure has a lot of friends around here," he said. "You're not the first to tell me to go easy on her."

The next morning, it was time to pay the fiddler for the dance. David was standing outside of Perley's door, on the raised concrete porch, the metal false-columns and the breaking of dawn behind him. He knocked loud enough should she be sleeping. Perley opened the door in a long lace and silk gown, the color of a brown egg's shell.

"What are you doin' here?" she looked angry, but mostly in shock. She had been crying. *Where was Roy? Why isn't someone here to drive me off and to protect her?*

"I'm here to say I'm sorry." David looked at her. There was no game to his looks, no flirtation, no disguise. He held tears in his eyes, and they didn't hold. They broke down his face, and he wiped them away in shame.

"Get in here." She pulled him by the arm and sat him down at the table. "I have to console you on top of it now?" She smiled and began to cry herself. "Son of a bitch," she cursed him. "Sons of bitches," she cursed the others. "My own," she said. She uncorked a bottle she had been drinking off of and poured them both a drink. It was sunrise, and they were drinking, and they each lit a smoke; the sun through the glass above the sink lit the streams of white that lifted and spread, and it felt right to be drinking and smoking in the morning.

David nearly waited for Perley to say something, but she just sucked her beautiful cheeks in with a long drag, exhaled, and stared out the window. It was David's job.

"I know a good lawyer in New York," David said. "I'll get him to help Clara out. I know it's little compensation. Believe it or don't, but I have fallen in love with your granddaughter."

"You fool," Perley said. "Don't you get it? No one wins anymore. Nothing lasts in the world." She took a drink, and David matched her. It tasted like Clara's hooch, but different. It was the same corn, but it was better crafted. A slight difference in mash bill, cooked at a better speed and heat—probably slower and with finer cuts getting to the tails, as this bourbon was not as "waxy," or oily, as Clara's.

161

"You were both hiding the corn from us," David said.

"No foolin'," Perley gave him a look. "You're outsiders, and it was our first date," she grinned, then frowned. The estate is larger than you would ever guess. Now it will go to dust." Her chest let go of its air, and her fine skin in her gown made David want to console himself and console her in one another's arms. He shook off the idea. "I want you to go now, young man," Perley said. "Finish that drink, and fly away." Was Perley always going to throw him out? David hoped he would find out, that this wouldn't be the last time he'd sit with Perley Stillwater.

"Perley, we want to protect your corn. We will talk with the historical society, and they might be willing to protect the old homestead and keep it going with the cornfields. I want to grow your corn on top of the IFDM building in Manhattan. It will be safe from GMO there, at least. We have a rooftop garden, and we'd like to keep the strain alive forever and secure that your species of corn will remain living proof of the 'original' American whiskey," David said. "I know this isn't much, but this will protect the homestead and the lineage of corn forever. Or for as long as possible," he said.

"What you do, you do because you need to sleep," Perley said. She sank into her seat, drank, and ground her cigarette into a blue glass ashtray. "We did it to live." David ground his into the smoker lamp stand ashtray. Perley coughed.

"Well, young David, at least it's something," she said. "You want to know about the corn you're drinkin' off right now?" Perley asked. Her neckline flexed, and the muscles of her jaw were taut as she took a sip. "By the way, how was your night in the cornfield?" Perley grinned. "See anything good?" she smiled.

"How did you know?" David asked. "Did you know all along about everything? The murder?" David stood up. The angel was close.

"Don't be a fool," Perley wiped her eyes. "Clara told me you broke into their house and that her brother hit you over the head. I didn't know about anything more than that, thank God, and I wish I never did. But I gave her the recipe to drug you," Perley grinned.

"Ha! Perley Stillwater." David sat down. He slugged back his drink. "I saw an old Native woman under the earth by a fire, chewing corn and spitting it into a pail, and she said 'Sula' to me. That was nearly all."

"You're not a Native American, David, but you do seem to pick up on whatever sprits are around." She nodded at him—a look to mean he was honorable. "That corn you're drinkin', that's corn from the Toltec tribes who broke off and wandered north for centuries. Their corn is the corn we use. They had a still they got from the Spanish. They carried it wherever they went, which was everywhere, as they were nomads. They would grow their corn, then after a harvest, pack up and leave. These people would chew the corn up and spit it out, then they would brew their whiskey with the chewed corn in their sacred still. They thought it was magic. It was, and it is." Perley winked at David. "OK, son, off!" Perley stood and pulled the chair David was sitting in from the back, and he felt how strong she was. He stood. The two hugged, and she held his face in her right hand and squeezed, all the way at his height, and she said something he did not understand. A blessing or a curse. It was both, likely.

"Out! Dubehash, you Yankee. Get out of Kentucky." Perley smiled. "You have more adventures to you." She smiled, and she started to cry. "I ought to kick your ass back to New York City. I ought to shoot you. I am going to get my gun, and she moved toward the stairs, leaving the door open, and he watched her climb the stairs and disappear. David played his part. He got in the Firebird and sped away, covering a few blocks and parking in front of the inn where Sam stood with the bags.

"Get what you were looking for?" Sam asked.

"Nope," said David. "Not so far."

CHAPTER THIRTY ONE

Parker's big old hound bayed as David drove up the drive, kicking a little dust. Sam looked at David, gave a younger man's grin, and pulled the emergency brake. The car slid a bit and dug its tires down into the gravel. David howled.

"I love that," Sam smiled. David still had a remnant buzz from Perley's hooch, but was legal to drive by a good ounce or two of moonshine. He scampered out of the car, did a strange little hop in the driveway and straightened up, slid a hand through his oily blond hair, went to the door, and summoned Parker.

Parker came to the door, the dog nipping at David's knees. "Hand over the keys, David." Parker grunted and showed his big white teeth. "I heard about what happened last night. Heard you told Lefevre to go easy on them too. You're all heart, sweet pea. Now give me back my Firebird." David handed the keys reluctantly, pulling them away once, and finally putting the ring right into Parker's old liver-spotted fist. "A-bliged," Parker grinned, and slapped the hand with the keys, finger tucked, onto David's shoulder. "You're quite a man for being such a boy at heart." Parker grimaced. "Let's get you two back where you belong."

They drove in the Firebird to Lexington.

Lefevre met them at the airport to say good-bye, a brace wrapped around his ribs. His son was with him, a good-looking boy, far better looking than Lefevre. Sam figured his friend in the FBI must have done well by marriage. Sam saddled over to give Lefevre a squeeze and poke him in the ribcage.

"This is my son, Jimmy Lefevre," Lefevre said, wincing.

Sam shook his head, "Jimmy, I have some unfinished business here. Maybe you can help me out with. See I can't leave Kentucky without tasting this Kentucky Bourbon Ale."

"Jesus, Sam," Parker said.

"Dugranval," Lefevre scorned.

"I'm in," David said. They all strolled into the airport bar with fifteen minutes to get their drinks.

"They mature this beer in ex-bourbon casks," Sam told the young man as they saddled up, and Sam ordered a beer each for the five of them. The beers arrived in snifters, which they weren't expecting, but which they realized was a smart choice by the barkeep, as the shape of the glass focused and amplified the aromas. "I can taste the sweet vanilla on the tip of my tongue," Jimmy said.

"That's all bullshit, you know," Sam said, much to the boy's surprise. "Sweet on the tip, bitter in the back, sour and salty on the sides. A misrepresentation of the sensitivity of the tongue. We've known since the '70s that the tongue map was worthless, but no one bothered to look up the truth." Sam was in teacher mode, prepping this Jimmy for class. "The German scientist who came up with it, Hanig, I believe, he wasn't even familiar with Japanese cuisine, and so he failed to include a fifth taste—umami—which is glutamate. You are most likely familiar with the commercialized version—MSG."

"There's also some debate about the existence of a sixth taste receptor for fat," David chimed in, but his thoughts were elsewhere. He finished his beer and knocked twice on the bar, signaling he wanted to wrap this show up.

"I know what fat tastes like," Parker said to no one in particular. "Fat tastes good." Parker laughed. No one else did.

The boy turned bashful, unable to come up with anything to say, but Sam could tell he was intrigued. "Listen," he said, and he shot a glance at Lefevre, "I expect to see an application from you for IFDM on my desk this winter. Deadline's December 10."

"Well, time's up!" Parker grinned. "Drink your beer, son. That's all you get! Your Pop is a teetotaler." Lefevre shot him a scowl.

Sam was in second class on the way back, thinking of Lydia again, giddy, imagining what he'd do with her when he got home. He'd hire a babysitter for the night—no, for the week. David was in first class, stretching out his long legs, trying not to think about Clara, but thinking about her all the same.

The plane lifted off, the cabin bucked, and Kentucky became a Kentucky of the mind.

CHAPTER THIRTY TWO

New York City was still showing off her flamboyant autumn. Life had gone on at IFDM in their absence, and Samuel Dugranval came back to a slew of papers awaiting his attention. It felt strange to be in this familiar spot, where there was no physical evidence that anything had happened at all, save the fading bruise beneath his eye. He couldn't work, so he looked at his watch. It would be two hours before Lydia would be back at the apartment; it felt like too much time to kill. Why did she have to have a dentist appointment today? Sam felt like his son after a long day—like a whiny, tired, hungry little boy.

Mrs. B. came on the intercom. "Sam, Mr. Barclay is on the line."

"Patch him in," Sam said, muddling the expression, exhausted but ready to give the good news.

"Are you sitting down?" Sam asked.

"Shoot," Barclay replied.

"I found a match on the corn used in your whiskey, and your whiskey is much older than we ever could have guessed. You've found a five-hundred-year-old piece of history that's capsizing our notions of the history of bourbon. With that bottle, you've not only stumbled upon a divine-tasting drink, you've opened up a whole new field of distillation studies. Thanks to you, I've got my work cut out for me for years."

"What? Woah! So you're saying it's worth something!"

"No price tag is too high."

"Ha!" Barclay went silent for a moment. "Well, Dugranval," he said, "I have a bit of a confession to make. I didn't just find that one bottle. I found a whole case. Well, nearly a whole case—one bottle was

missing—but I've got eleven bottles sitting out here in my Patriot safe."
Sam nearly choked on his spit.

"Eleven bottles? What—" Sam stopped short.

"Of course, I should turn them over to the Port Authority. They own the land after all—it's just, well it seems like such a waste, who knows where they'll end up."

"Listen," Sam's mind was spinning fast. "I have a proposition for you. How about you forget about my consultation fees. I have a buddy over at AKRF, the archaeological consulting firm that works with the Lower Manhattan Development Corporation. Why don't you give him the bottles. He'll take care of all the legal stuff, and trust me, that bourbon will end up in the right hands. We can get a few donated to IFDM, some to the Oscar Getz Museum in Bardstown, and I'll make sure the rest go to the Native American Historical Society of New York." He paused. "And of course, if you happen to tell my friend that you only found ten bottles, well I wouldn't report anything to the contrary."

Barclay laughed. "You're quite a guy Dugranval. Quite a guy. And, Sam, thank you." There was the sound of backhoes and drills. "Listen, I've got to fly. Got a foundation to dig. Send me your friend's info." There was static, and the line dropped. Sam was left holding the phone to his ear, listening to the sound of nothing left for him to do. Lydia would be upset, of course. They were no better off with Leo's tuition check than they had been a week ago, plus he had spent no small sum on the hotel and airfare and all that gas David burned up in the Firebird chasing his girl.

David, too, was worse for the wear. Between a broken heart and the savings he'd vowed to dole out to a proper lawyer for Clara, he and Sam were a regular old pair of romantic fools.

Sam leaned back in his chair, cast an eye across his bookshelves, and sighed. He reached into his breast pocket and pulled out the letter that had been burning a hole there all week.

"Professor Dugranval," it read in English, despite the kanji on the envelope, "I hope all is well and hope you share my sentiment when I say, 'Let bygones be bygones.' Perhaps it strikes you as odd that I would be writing after such a long silence, but something terribly important has come up, something only you can help me with. I cannot give the details here, but I need you to come immediately to Japan. Sincerely, Tado Ehime Koga"

The Sulfur, thought Sam. Never would he help that kid again. But still…

Epilogue

FDM emptied out, and Sam remained in his chair. He stared at his bookshelves and imagined writing a history. It would be the untold story of bourbon—the Stillwater corn and the Native Americans who traveled with that corn for hundreds of years. It would begin with the Spaniards bringing a gorgeous alembic still to the United States.

Imagine five hundred years. *Is it possible to imagine five hundred years?* It was a time span the body could never understand, a wisdom impossible to Sam—but a window had been opened, and he'd had a glance. The title, *hmmm,* "A New History of Bourbon: Spit in The Kettle and Nomadic Distillation in the New World."

He indulged for a moment in all that the title implied. But what could he possibly pin down? Had this five-hundred-year-old bourbon been stored first in the guttural sacks of grassland beasts and tied at the hips of the women as they walked? Or had it been placed in clay jars and carried by men, sacred and revered in its place among the hierarchy of the clan, in the flanks of their wandering formations? Could this explain the deep red color of Barclay's find?

Stories. How many stories happened in five hundred years? A tribe alone, but coming into contact with others: new men from the sea, old tribes from the north. The tribe would be driven different ways, and they would drive others out of their path. There would be attack; there would be trade. Of course Sam would have to come up with evidence, but for now, he was dreaming. For now, he was interested in the story.

Sam remembered David's arrowheads: the Toltec had wars with tribes bigger than them, tribes skilled at hunting bigger game. They had pushed on, there was blood, family, corn, and whiskey. Meat.

Marriage. And there were politics wherever people were found. Some politicians would want their booze someday. Sam knew facts about this: How whiskey was a currency, how votes in early America were bought with booze. Perhaps word got around that these Toltec's had the best hooch. They were a legend then, but they had become a legend lost. Imagine the disappearing and reappearing of history. A whisper among the whites in the old West outside of some outpost town. A band of native people brewing hooch in a magic still. With a gallon of hooch, Washington was known to have secured two votes, but the Toltec whiskey would be worth far more. A few bottles perhaps were sent East. A case to New York City. A friend of a friend out there in politics, someone who knew the legend, a Kentucky trapper perhaps, a man of fur and pelts with connections to a rum runner with a ship.

But something had gotten in the way of the story. Some turn of sail, a storm, high winds, a broken mast, and history was lost. The earth of Manhattan began to fill. Shoes. cherry pits, animal bones—the past was paved over by progress and politics, larger wars between larger tribes, the boom of the mighty dollar, and an excavator who ran machines to make room. It was impossible. The world held too much; time took so much away.

And yet, something had remained. Even as time constantly erased and men built the world anew, something had remained. A case of whiskey had survived. Two women in a small town backed up against forest and field had kept a story alive. The tribe had all but disappeared, but their wisdom had remained, buried among the castoffs of culture, until tragedy or luck let it air.

It was in the wake of this discovery, in an office at the Institute of Fermentation, Distillation, and Maturation on Manhattan's Upper West Side, that a middle-aged Frenchman—broke, exhausted, and with a throb in his shoulder—considered all that had passed.

Recipes

Old Fashioned:

2 oz Rittenhouse Rye 100 proof

½-oz simple syrup

2 dashes Angostura bitters

Orange wheel with zest ribbon

Whiskey-soaked cherry

Place the orange wheel in the bottom of a rocks glass with the cherry, dangling the zest ribbon over the rim. Add the bitters. Gently press all until juicy. Add the rye, then slowly mix in the simple syrup. Add ice and adjust the orange ribbon.

The Russian Caravan:

2 oz Elijah Craig Small Batch Bourbon, 12 Year Old

2 oz Russian (smoked) tea

½-oz lemon juice

½-oz honey syrup

½-oz Saint Germain elderflower liqueur

Club soda

Lemon zest

Shake all ingredients and pour over fresh ice in a highball glass. Top with club soda and garnish with the lemon zest.

~ Enjoy… and please drink responsibly. ~